SAFEKEEPING

SAFEKEEPING

Jonellen Heckler

G. P. Putnam's Sons
New York

PRINTED IN THE UNITED STATES OF AMERICA

For my husband
Lou
and my son
Steven

FORT BENJAMIN HARRISON

INDIANAPOLIS, INDIANA

CHAPTER 1

Tuesday, May 9, 1972

JUDY GREER thought she heard a noise. It was a rustling or a scraping or both, coming to her down the long, vertical cylinder of sleep. Echoing.

She jolted awake. The skin of her face ballooned hot and full, stretching with adrenaline. She listened.

There were a thousand such incidents in her captive existence: the imagined nighttime creak, the prowler of unknown and evil intent. Such terrors haunt every mystery story in the world. Surely this one was not real.

There. It came again, down on the first floor. Outside? A scratching. A moving or removing. She lay stiffly in her bed, trying to decipher the sounds, but the roaring of pulse in her ears began to interfere.

With great difficulty, she rolled onto her stomach and pressed her face into the sheet. Her hand found the edge of the mattress and clutched it.

The fragrance of her bedclothes reminded her that she alone would have to answer. Always. For in this bed there was the scent of only one person. Self. That person upon whom she had to rely perpetually.

And so she got up.

This would be the last time for the agonizing routine of hiding and then facing the elusive enemy; of hearing noises and finding nothing. This time there really was a prowler. And she would kill him.

She would aim at the eyes. She wanted to see them grow wide with recognition. She wanted him to know, as though he could pass the message along to all the nameless devils, that she could no longer be tormented. That she had had enough.

9

Judy lifted the cold revolver from a dresser drawer and moved through its rituals like someone listening to an unseen teacher. This cartridge here, that cocking there. The light from the window conspired to help her: a streetlamp, part of a moon. The little metallic clicks fed her resolve.

She no longer tried to make sense of what happened day by day; there were no more attributions to God's plan or man's error. Events simply piled up, inscrutable and mute. If once Judy had known the Why of the world, she had forgotten now what it was.

Twelve-year-old Kevin Greer gently pushed the kitchen window up as far as he could and waited. Crouching down in a bed of dry leaves, he put his shoulder to the brick wall and listened for his mother. She would be sure to catch him sneaking back in, and then there would be no TV for a week. Or worse?

It was chilly. Damn. Well, no sense putting it off. He had been out long enough, sitting at the edge of the post green, backside freezing on an old cannon. Lord, it was good to get out, to feel the open world. Lately the air in his home had become unbearably scarce, as if a noose had been set against his collarbone. To climb out, to run in the night, was to take heart.

He had been running free a lot in the past few weeks, using various windows for escape hatches. His mother seemed to sleep soundly, hadn't missed him yet.

Kevin grasped the kitchen sill, heaved himself up and leaned onto the counter beside the sink. So far, so good. Now a knee. Now a foot. The can opener was in the way. He slid it over.

Judy held the revolver in front of her like a shield, murderous anger coursing through her limbs. Nothing could touch her now.

Slowly. Slowly. She crept toward the kitchen, stalking the point of entry. She would be methodical. He expected whimpering. He would get lead.

Her only regret was the darkness. She wanted to see his alarm. But to hit the light would be to give warning. The kitchen door on the hall side was closed; the one on the dining room side stood open. Judy circled silently to it. Stopped. Squinted.

A shadow lurched in front of the shiny window square. The remaining scraps of doubt left her. This person had definitely crawled through the window. He was still on the counter.

He saw her too late. There was an explosion and a stream of fire hurtling toward him. He fell, chin and chest first, onto the linoleum slab. Pain gurgled in his throat. Shards of glass sang everywhere, raining down on him.

He fell again. Through the floor. Through the basement. Through the molten earth.

Then he sailed suddenly up, into a starry hole, and out across the wind.

CHAPTER 2

KEVIN FOCUSED on the bottle that floated over him. It was held by a hand. The hand belonged to a man who ran beside him. Kevin was gliding quickly along on his back. He recognized the rose-strewn wallpaper that went by.

They passed his living room. Where were they going? Kevin slipped out the front doorway. Frigid air smacked his face. He became aware of physical agony so steep that it reached up from his bowels to rip parts of him away from their moorings. Nerves and muscles tore, let go, sagged and dangled by single electric strands. He cried out.

He was tilting now, feet downward. Light pulsed in steady rhythm across his eyes. They turned him around and shoved him headfirst into a van. People bundled in coats stood in the street, staring at him. He could tell by the mournful pitch and staccato cadence of their tones that he was in trouble. Serious trouble. What had happened?

His mother climbed frantically into the van. The doors closed. Her visible fear alarmed him. He had always gauged situations by her expression. It never lied. Now it was openmouthed with gasps, white and wide-eyed with apprehension. Her long wheat-colored hair, which usually flipped cleanly this way and that, hung in damp clumps. She was wearing her green bathrobe. Her bathrobe!

Fire and flying glass astounded his memory.

She had shot him.

For crawling in the window?

Panic welled up under his breastbone and grew into the point of a knife against his heart. She didn't love him anymore. He had watched it coming.

He was going to vomit. He tried to speak it, but his lips felt large and heavy. Hot liquid began to pour violently from his nose and mouth, stinging him, choking him. The attendant gently turned Kevin's head and tried to help him with a towel. The ambulance shivered and began to move.

In the first seconds of consciousness he was three years old, passing through the night toward some new place; lulled to sleep and then smiling into wakefulness with the car's trembling speed; listening to the lilting, whispered happiness of his parents. His mother still loved him. He knew because she crooned *"little boy, little boy,"* at every bedtime as they tipped slowly back and forth in the rocker, the carpet whishing under them.

The doors clanged open. They pulled him out. He couldn't feel his body anymore. They must have given him something.

He looked for the green bathrobe. It was here. And the familiar aroma of his mother's perfume. That fragrance always reminded him of the other one, the joyful one who had melted gradually away from him into her deepest self.

Now she had hurt him. Why? A stark sense of abandonment rapidly filled his chest, crushing his lungs.

She mustn't see. That was the worst thing after all. The worst. To upset her brought disaster. Anytime he had spoken about his sorrow, there were awesome consequences: the stunned frown as she came to understand the texture of his emptiness, and then the sudden sound of her own grieving.

No. He would eat his feelings before he would let them out. For whenever he spoke his mind, her anguish was set loose. And it was always more terrible than his.

Major Thomas Wellington eased his car into a tight parking space at Methodist Hospital and cut the engine. His clothes were limp with perspiration. He had yanked them on hurriedly when Judy called, jumping around, stuffing his feet into shoes, shoving his wallet and handkerchief into his pockets, bumping into things, cursing.

Bless his wife. Donna loved Judy, too, and had run outside in her nightclothes to warm up the car while he staggered about. By the time he arrived at the post hospital Kevin had been moved downtown to Methodist.

Now he slammed the car door and ran toward the square of light that was Methodist's emergency entrance. Wind flew up his sleeves and pants legs, tingling against the moisture on his skin.

Damn it. He had told them and told them that she might do something like this. His memos on the subject had passed from his superior officer into military oblivion. They didn't approve of her, of course, but that was no excuse. Their obligation was to support her to the best of their ability until her husband came home.

The corridors were empty except for a lone woman behind glass at the admitting desk. She didn't look up. He strode past her, following the Emergency Room signs. Its doors were propped open.

"Just a minute, sir!"

He wheeled around. It was the woman from the admitting desk.

"How may I help you?"

"I'm looking for a patient, Kevin Greer. And his mother."

"Yes. They're in Emergency. Are you a relative?"

"I'm . . ." He fumbled in his pocket for his military ID. "Major Thomas Wellington, the family assistance officer for Mrs. Greer." He found the laminated card and showed it to her.

"Well." She studied him doubtfully.

"Mrs. Greer is the wife of a prisoner of war; her husband, Major Ronald Greer, is in North Vietnam. I represent the Army. I help Mrs. Greer with whatever she needs. She called me."

The lines of concern creasing her forehead relaxed. She gestured toward the Emergency Room. "Go right ahead."

He walked around the corner and saw Judy at once. Jesus! She was in her bathrobe, the front of it was splotched with blood. Her shoulder-length honey hair tangled wildly, and the round, appealing face held a stunned gaze. He reached out his hands. She came to him. They met in the center of the room, oblivious to the white-coated figures brushing by.

"It was an accident," she apologized. A throatful of tears muffled her words.

"Of course." She didn't need to tell him she wouldn't shoot her own kid! "Where is he?"

"In there." She pointed at one of the examining rooms. "They don't want me to get in the way. There are so many nurses. Everybody's working. He's not . . . awake."

He drew her gently into a corner. "How bad is it?"

"I don't know. His arm, for sure."

Their breaths were warm on each other's faces. They stood inside an invisible circle. He cared so much for Judy and for Kevin. Nothing romantic—no, no! He could say it with total honesty. He and Donna both felt deep friendship and admiration for Judy. She was sterling: a beautiful bird impaled by an arrow. Her suffering was justified, profound. And she had endured it with grace.

It had started out as a duty, this taking care of Judy and Kevin. Now he could never turn it loose even if the Army reassigned him. He, too, had felt the pain of the arrow.

"Can we get a Coke?"

"Yes." She led the way to a small lab room where tubes and machines cluttered the counters. A red soft-drink machine hulked in a corner.

They sat close together on hard plastic chairs, he trying to maintain a pose of strength for her, she looking small and puzzled. Had she lost weight recently, or was it just the posture of defeat?

He studied her profile in silence. On a good day she had merry eyes. They were a dark, probing brown, a window to her sensitive intelligence. Her brows arched regally over them. The lips were slender, but bowed to perfection. They could pucker in whimsy or pull suddenly into a generous straight-toothed smile.

This never should have happened, this sliding back and sliding back on her part until something had to give. The Army should have helped her. It had been like watching the print fade from curtains in a sunny window, like feeling the last wisp of fresh air in a sealed room stop moving and use itself up until the candle flickered out. And with the gradual fading, an unpredictable resentment had begun to possess Judy, to mushroom in the hollow spaces of her life. A rage. Most of it had spilled into a compelling energy for the antiwar effort. His favorite memory of Judy was a TV news clip showing her being removed from the Capitol steps, still in a prone position. She lay on her side, leaning on one elbow, ankles nonchalantly crossed. The men with gray shirts and badges had picked her up just like that—an unblinking, very pretty statue—and carted her to a paddy wagon. Guts. He liked that about her. Every morning when he put on his Army uniform, he thought of that incident. That was the day he had decided she was right. His Army-issue shirt and tie had not been comfortable since.

"Mrs. Greer?" A doctor appeared at the threshold. His name tag said "Randall." He was frowning.

Judy gave Tom a fearful glance, and he followed her into the hallway, stood at her elbow. She looked toward the examining room door, which was still closed.

"How is he?" Judy's skin was waxen white. Her lower lip had a bluish cast.

"Conscious. He should be all right."

"Oh, thank God! Oh!" She put her fingers to her mouth for a moment. "Can I see him? I want to be with him."

"In a minute. We've started a transfusion. He needs X rays, and then we'll move him into surgery to stitch the arm. Luckily the bullet missed the bone." Randall jammed his hands into the pockets of his lab coat and tilted his chin until he looked down the length of his nose at Judy. "You know I'll have to put in a police report." His tone was accusing, edged with disgust.

"I thought so."

The doctor seemed suddenly aware of Tom and glared at him as if demanding an explanation for his presence.

Tom offered a handshake, but it was ignored. "I'm Tom Wellington, Mrs. Greer's assistance officer and her attorney."

"Assistance officer?"

"Mrs. Greer's husband is a prisoner in North Vietnam. I am assigned by the Army to help her with legal and other matters."

"I see." Randall tried to look down his nose at Tom, but Tom was tall enough to be on eye level. They regarded each other coldly.

"Where else is he hurt?" Judy begged.

"His arm's the only serious injury we've found so far, but I've ordered tests. The spill he took may have caused some damage. His chin was bleeding. We patched it up."

The examining room door opened, and four or five nurses and orderlies wheeled Kevin quickly out and along the corridor, away from them. His eyes were shut tight.

Judy sucked in her breath.

"You can go with him to X ray."

Tom started off with Judy, but the doctor tapped his shoulder. "Just the mother," he said.

They carefully steered Kevin around a corner, and then Tom couldn't see them anymore.

"Please wait by the desk. A police officer will be here shortly to take a statement." The doctor walked away.

A statement. Shit! There would be all kinds of red tape. Well, he could get her off the hook. It was an accident, for Pete's sake. Anyone could see that.

While he was waiting, Tom tried to think of the happy times, the times when Judy and Kevin still ambled around Fort Harrison on a rusty bicycle built for two, when they laughed and lay on their backs in the summer grass of the post green at the band concerts, when they hugged unabashedly. When had it stopped? There was no one day or month that came to him circled in red. Their love had never stopped. Of that he felt sure. But the hugging and the talking had.

They were so fetchingly similar, Judy and Kevin: steel bones and agile, athletic frames. They were action figures drawn with a sharp charcoal pencil on new paper. Kevin could throw and catch a ball with boys half again his age. But lately his confidence had waned. Voltage was missing.

How could Tom have saved them? What could he do next? He had tried and tried, but she would have none of it. Tonight's call was the first from her in more than a year, even though he routinely touched base with her once a week. She asked him for nothing, politely refused most social invitations from Donna. It bewildered him because he perceived a flowing affection beneath her aloofness. Perhaps his uniform was the enemy.

He'd suggested to Judy countless times that the post psychiatrist might be able to help her.

Maybe now she'd say yes.

CHAPTER 3

Thursday, June 8, 1972

KEVIN EYED the psychiatrist thoughtfully. He seemed so friendly, this man. But Kevin knew it was a trick. They were trying to get him to say things that would hurt his mother. They wanted to punish her for the shooting, and they hadn't been able to get her into jail; Major Wellington had outsmarted them.

He would be careful in his answers. He wouldn't let them take her away from him. It had been a mistake, but they just couldn't see it that way. This was an Army psychiatrist after all, and Kevin knew what the Army thought of his mother.

His world was cursed with hateful stares. Everyone took sides. The kids his age let it fly at him in school—that public school he had to go to. He wished Fort Harrison had its own school. That might save him from some of it. Kids spit at him down the stairwells at school and ripped the pages out of his books. People either hated the war and felt his dad deserved to be captured, or they loved the war and hated his mother because of her peace marches. He got it daily from both sides.

"You were in the kitchen," the psychiatrist was saying.

Kevin blinked at him.

"And what were you doing in the kitchen?"

"Getting ready to make a sandwich."

The psychiatrist looked disappointed. "Now, Kevin," he said softly, "is that the truth?"

Silly. Why had he said that? This man would know differently.

"No."

"You were doing what then?"

"I was ... I was ... coming in through the kitchen window."

"All right. And where had you been?"

"Out."

"Can you be more specific?"

"Just out, running around. You know."

"Why is that?"

"Just to be ... out."

"And you had gone out a lot, on other nights?"

"Yes."

"Your mother had heard you some of those nights. Did you know that? She was frightened. She thought it was a prowler."

Kevin shrugged. Better not to comment on anything about his mother.

"When you came in the window, do you remember what happened?"

Kevin's wound tingled. The muscles of his arm began to jump. "No."

"Nothing? You don't remember anything after you came in the window?"

The sun split apart. A holocaust. He could feel it sear his skin. The brightness. He closed his eyes.

"No."

"Let's talk about something else," the psychiatrist said sympathetically, walking around the desk to sit in his vinyl rolling chair. "Do you remember your father?"

Did he? *Father.* A man's head appeared in the dim well of Kevin's mind: unmoving, totally black and white. His standard vision.

"Do you?"

"I don't know."

"Why don't you think? I'll wait while you think."

Kevin thought. The man was still black and white, shiny. His eyes were not looking at Kevin but off somewhere to the right. Kevin scratched his stomach, waited.

That was the trouble. All this over someone he could

hardly remember. It could have been anybody. A visitor. Brief memories, like nursery rhymes, had come to Kevin from time to time—stilted, always the same. Were they things that really happened or things he had been told?

"Did you find anything yet?"

Kevin held up a finger. He would bring out the scraps of film and run them for this man. It wouldn't upset anything. It would satisfy him; he could write it down on the thin paper in his folder, write it with the black fountain pen that leaked ink onto his first two fingers. That would make him feel he had done his job.

One of the pictures was very pleasant. Yes, this would be a good one to tell. Kevin and his father, rolling over and over and over, down a snowy hill. Lying on their backs, laughing into a gray, sparkling sky.

"I remember something."

The man's chair creaked as he leaned forward in interest.

"We were rolling down a snowy hill, my dad and I. It was funny. We were laughing. We did it a lot of times."

"Good," the psychiatrist said, nodding encouragement. "Do you remember any feelings you had about him?"

He had played the scene so often the feelings were hardly there anymore. Like gum you had chewed for a long time. The flavor had gone. "I liked him."

"Anything else?"

His father sliding a boot onto Kevin's foot in a shoe store! This scene had words. It wasn't like the other one where all they did was laugh. The boots were important. Expensive. And he wanted them desperately.

"But what about the brown shoes Mama told us to get?" Kevin asked, worried, pointing to the oxfords that rested in a box.

"We'll get those, too." His father smiled—an adoring smile— and patted him heavily on the cheek. "You gotta have boots, partner. Nobody ever heard of a cowpoke without boots."

"Daddy! Can I wear them home?"

"You bet." His dad pushed the other boot over his sock, and Kevin stood up, a real cowboy. Fancy. Tough.

"He bought me some cowboy boots. We were supposed to get Sunday shoes, but we got both. I was happy."

"That's a nice one." The psychiatrist smiled. "What else do you see?"

There were a couple more good ones in there. But the psychiatrist said, "Anything bad? Anything you don't like to remember?"

A web fell suddenly across Kevin's face and clung there.

"Do you want to talk about it?"

The back of Kevin's head began to pulse achingly. *His mother and father crying in their bed.* He could hear them. He crept to the door and listened. Parents didn't cry! It terrified him. Was it because his father was going on a trip? No, that was nothing to cry about. A trip was a good thing.

They were whispering together. His father began to sob in deep, cracked tones; he blew his nose, his breath shuddering loudly in his throat. Kevin ran back to bed and huddled under the covers, seeking the warm spot he hoped would still be in the center of his mattress. He lay against it, trying to draw comfort from it as it cooled.

He had an image of a uniformed man waving at the top of some stairs, next to a greenish airplane. His father? The bill of the cap shaded his eyes. Kevin wasn't sure that he really remembered the final good-bye. But he did remember pressing his face into his father's sleeve as they drove to the airfield, trying to get and keep the scent of his father's strength and affection. The hairiness. The maleness. His father smelled clean and powerful. He oozed with secrets. Good secrets. Riches. Things to be shared. Excitement. And each secret had an aroma.

Long after his dad was gone, Kevin kept in touch with him by lingering in his closet, inhaling man fragrance from left-behind clothes. But as the months passed, air stole the reassuring smells. Jackets and shirts became colorless, limp.

They dried out. Died.

"Did you think of something?" the psychiatrist urged.

"No."

Monday, July 17, 1972

NOW SHE HAD gone too far. She could see it on the psychiatrist's face. During the six weeks of her therapy she had increasingly forgotten that Ron belonged to the Army and that it would always act in his best interest. He was more valuable than she. The preservation of Judy Greer would be attempted only because the preservation of Ronald Greer was essential.

She hadn't intended to talk so much. But this What's-His-Name—Major Hooper—had led her compassionately from one subject to another, from one admission to another. She had stepped without hesitation from stone to stone in the midst of a placid stream, only to look up and find herself perilously far from safety.

"Go on."

Anyone would feel as you do, he had said. *You have a million reasons for feeling frustrated and sad. Tell me some of the ideas you have for trying to feel better.* And she had spun them out . . . all the tentative half thoughts.

She wanted to build a good home life for her son, she told him. She wanted to destroy her home and run away. She wanted a divorce. She wanted to wait angelically, to be chaste, be the perfect POW wife working in harmony with the military. She wanted to stop the American war machine, throwing herself bodily into the wheels and cogs, causing them to groan to a halt. She wanted a no-strings affair. She wanted her husband back. The range of her wishes ignored logic, but each one alone was logical. And all were possibilities—except for the one about sitting quietly by, exhibiting faith. That was the one Judy could never settle for.

"Do you want to go on?" The psychiatrist struck a relaxed pose in a side chair. None of this behind-the-desk business for him, Judy thought. He would close the gap, lure her into his confidence. Indeed he had.

Fear began to speak to her from a corner of the room. Words of caution. The Army would find her daydreams serious threats. She was talking to a presence as loyal to Ronald Greer as his own mother and father. A wife wouldn't tell her husband's parents that she wanted to leave him or cheat on him. Especially when the husband was in no position to defend himself. It would be up to the parents, then, to defend their son.

"Nothing?" Hooper consulted his watch.

"What time is it?"

"Almost time to finish up." He gave her an understanding smile. "Would you like to quit for today?"

"I can't think of anything else."

"Your fantasies, do they alarm you?" The voice was kind. Had she imagined his disapproval?

Well ... it didn't matter. Ronald Greer might be the Army's man, but they could not control Judy. She was plainly out of their reach.

CHAPTER 4

Saturday, August 12, 1972

"DID YOU TELL him you're horny as hell?" Susan Benson was not one to mince words. She had an exterior to match: all showy colors and vivid makeup. Not vulgar, in Judy's estimation. Just suggestive.

"What does it matter, Susan? What's he going to do, throw himself on the altar of my passion?"

Of the few things that kept Judy alive after five years as society's misfit, Susan was an important one. Her dabs of crudeness had just enough realism to remind Judy of the old days, before she became a saint and people began to speak reverently to her.

Susan finished stirring the instant coffee and smacked it onto her kitchen table in two aged mugs. Everything she possessed, including her person, looked well used. She plunked into a chair opposite Judy and pointed a finger.

"You almost killed your kid. Thank God you only winged him. Now you've spent the whole summer in analysis with this Army Freud and you haven't told him diddley."

Judy flinched. It wasn't true. She had told him a great deal. About the accident and why she fired the . . . Even Kevin had consented to a private session. More than one. No one could say they hadn't agreed to have help.

"You're telling yourself, 'It's not so.' But, Judy, you haven't changed a bit. You're losing your grip on it. If I know you, you walked in there wearing your military-wife decorum and that mother-in-law of yours perched on your shoulder like a conscience."

Couldn't Susan ever tiptoe? Instantly Judy felt the urge to quit Susan, to dump her down the sink with the coffee.

She got up from the table and poured the black liquid into the rusting drain.

Quit. Some days quit was everything. She had ignored the League of Families and dropped Waiting Wives, sawing off the cancerous limbs to save her life. They reminded her of who she was, and she had decided not to be reminded. She jerked the back door open.

"Wait, wait!" Susan leaped up to press her hand against it, trying to shut it again. "Don't go, Judy. We'll talk. I won't tell you, you tell me. You tell me, okay?" Susan was breathless, her three pendants bobbing against her throat. One was a gold heart her husband, Bink, had given her in April, before he left for a routine tour of duty in Korea. Major Jeffrey Benson: another spouse catapulted down the rabbit hole by Army orders. *She's alone now, too,* Judy thought. *She knows some of it. A taste of it.*

Judy allowed Susan to close the door. The slam set off the distant barking of dogs, probably in one of the bedrooms. Susan boarded and groomed terriers, right in her home. A *lot* of terriers. Judy started to laugh.

"Now you're going to get hysterical." Susan grinned. "Something about the dogs, right?"

"You'll let them loose. Send them after me like hounds. I *can't* leave." A million places tickled wildly under her ribs. Was she going to wet herself?

They sat at the table again.

Judy sobered. "Okay, here it is. I love Ron. But I want a divorce."

Susan leaned forward. "You want a divorce?" she whispered. "Are you sure?"

Judy was sure. She had thought it all out. Limbo was the place she didn't want to be anymore. She would end it. Because there was no end in sight.

"But they're talking peace. It's almost over."

"They're always talking peace. It'll never end. I believe that."

"It would be a terrible shock for Ron," Susan said, "to come home to that. A *fait accompli.*"

But there was no guilt left in Judy. She had overdosed on guilt, had eaten it on her bread, mixed it into her salad every day for five years. It smiled from the television. It came out of the shower head. It rose odorously from each new pair of shoes. *Ron doesn't have. Ron can't.*

"Well, it's honest. You wanted honest. There it is."

One of the dogs sent up a howl so piercing that both women stood up.

"Crap," Susan fumed, leading the way back down the hall. "They're always at it." She opened a bedroom door, and gray terriers tumbled out, whining, bumping against Judy's ankles, the walls and each other. They scattered, ran away through the rooms, yipping.

The sound made her think of men in torture. No! What had she said? Images of twisted faces flew at her like bats. She put up her hands instinctively.

"Judy?" Susan peered at her through undulating water.

"I still love him," she gasped. Maybe by calling the words back into her mouth, she could prevent his pain. For she now remembered something she had always known. How could she have forgotten? She alone was responsible for Ron's welfare. Speaking against him set up malicious vibrations in his sphere. His captors were suddenly reminded of their hatred for this blue-eyed American major, lying alone in his cell. Her feelings agitated them. They turned their heads in his direction. *He sat up from the floor in fear. There would be footsteps soon.*

It was only by the good thoughts, the positive, the courageous thoughts that she could protect him.

"Did you tell that Freud you wanted a divorce?" Susan and Judy were running down the street, each being pulled by three terriers on leashes. The August day curved over them: broad, supple leaves and silver sky.

"I told him," Judy rasped, lungs burning in the effort to keep up with Susan.

"Jeez! Why did you do that?" One of the dogs stopped to

sniff a mailbox post, and Susan turned to confront Judy. "The Army'll hate that."

"It's not their business to love it or hate it." Judy watched impassively as one of the terriers lifted his leg and yellow liquid splashed against the post.

"Well," Susan said, "you can expect a lot of trouble." She looked nervously toward the nearest house lest the owner of the mailbox be rocking on the front porch. "Okay, mutts," she ordered, tugging at the dogs. "Let's give somebody else's lawn a turn."

Susan's attitude puzzled Judy. It wasn't up to the Army after all. It was personal.

"It's not their business," Judy said again, trying to catch up as Susan drifted from side to side, towed by her three charges. "Anyway, they won't know it until I file. What you tell a psychiatrist is confidential."

"Good luck."

A Doberman tied to a porch railing growled at the terriers and jumped wildly back and forth, straining at his rope. "That's all we need. Here, let's cross the street." Susan took the leashes from Judy and walked the six dogs herself. It was impossible to get close to her. Each terrier had taken it as a personal mission to tell the Doberman how to behave. There was a strident chorus of yapping and a few officious barks.

Judy passed Susan and jogged along in front of her, looking back. "What are they going to do, get me with a poison dart?"

This struck Susan funny. Both women started to giggle. Judy loved to hear Susan's laughter. It was raucous; every tooth in her head showed. "I can see it all now," Susan raved, in a mood to act it out. She blew an invisible dart in Judy's direction. Judy played along, grabbing her neck with a grimace and tumbling into the grass.

"You think I'm kidding," Susan said, standing over her.

Judy blinked into the sunlight, getting a tilted vision of Susan against scattered clouds. Susan of the shiny pink blouse and snug slacks was your stock come-what-may military wife: Rip down the curtains, and here we go. She went at it with zest. Home was anyplace Susan happened to be. She had her own turtlelike shell and no need of another roof.

Susan lived inside a sturdy body: round everything. Not fat, just round. She was a series of tight circles. Judy remembered drawing animals this way in eighth-grade art class—a circle for the head, circles for the chest, circles for the rump and so on. Susan stood with her feet apart, adding to the impression that it would take a lot to knock her over.

The dogs breathed loudly in Judy's ears, restlessly nudging her, occasionally drooling from their slim, curled tongues.

"You're running amuck, girl," Susan said as Judy got to her feet.

"I guess it takes amuck to know amuck," she answered good-naturedly.

Susan smiled. "No kidding now. You haven't exactly endeared yourself to the Pentagon with your peace marching and all that."

"The war is a mishandled mess."

Susan held up her hand for silence. "The peace marching. The accident. And now she wants a divorce. Do you know what that would do, Judy? You've already become an official embarrassment."

Judy, stung, turned her back on Susan and walked slowly toward home.

"Okay, okay," Susan shouted, with the sound of twenty-four paws muffling her plea. "You talk, I'll listen."

Judy kept her pace.

"I'm just telling you, they'll try to prevent it. It would destroy Ron. They can't afford to have a guy like him on the emotional recovery list for very long. There's hardly anybody who knows what he knows about China. They'll be plugging him into Nixon's new diplomacy as soon as he gets here," Susan called. "He's too damned valuable to be sidelined by a divorce."

Judy wanted to go home, but her purse was inside Susan's house. She sat on Susan's front steps to wait.

The Indiana summer was gliding past. In spite of its beauty, it held a sameness for Judy as thick and unending as the hundreds of miles of corn that stretched away from Indianapolis in every direction. Soon the bitter winter would come and frost would creep in on the door latch. There was a strangeness of numbers about this place. Not just the ocean of amber corn, row upon row, dimpling, passing its ripeness, but the geese, which came in long dark ribbons, filling the migrant flyways with swift, purposeful flapping and casting shadow after shadow, like bruises on the earth. The mindless locust hordes, blackening the Indy roads with leaping confusion, brittle bodies propelled as if by mechanical spring. Locusts, crunch-crunching against startled windshields.

And the flatness. The feeling of living on an ancient map. The fear of sailing too far and dropping over the edge.

But this is where Ron had left her. And so she had stayed.

Susan came around the corner, hair fanning out in single strands around her concerned look. The dogs jostled her and tangled their leashes through her feet as she walked.

"You waited."

"I'm waiting for my purse."

"I've got a big mouth," Susan apologized as she unlocked the front door, unsnapped the leashes from six collars. "You want to talk some more or just split?"

"Split."

Susan crossed the high-ceilinged living room, picked up Judy's purse and brought it to her. Then, stepping into the noontime glare, she put a hand on Judy's arm. "Why do you want a divorce?"

Judy shrugged.

Susan followed her down the narrow cement path to the sidewalk. "Hey, why are you always running away? Is it sex?" Susan asked sympathetically. "Is that what it'll get you?"

Silence.

"You're too principled, kid."

"Now that's just crazy," Susan announced, licking the salty edge of a margarita glass. The women were lying head beside feet in a two-person Mexican hammock strung between maple trees in Susan's yard. Judy had finished her third margarita and was happily watching the hammock strings blur.

"You've gotta stop that purity nonsense." Susan held the glass over the side of the lightly swinging cradle. "Nobody expects you to be abstaining." She took a long slurp of her drink, sat up and put her feet over the edge to brush the ground. "If that's the only thing you're missing . . ."

"It's not," Judy said defensively.

Susan stood up, and began to tap the hammock gently, lolling Judy back and forth. "Take it easy. Let me tell you a bedtime story. About a lonely military wife whose husband is far, far away."

"Is that you? Or me?"

"It's anybody," Susan replied, looking into the distance for a vision of the next act. "She's very lonely. But she finds out a secret. A secret that can help her through. While all the good husbands are away, doing their good duty for the entire world, the good husbands whose turn it is to stay home at old Fort Whatever take care of all the wives. Not just their own."

Electricity began to snake through Judy's spine. Careful. Consider the source. Susan had a definitely racy aura.

"None of them are bad. They're all good—all the husbands and the wives. But they get lonely. And, when it's their turn to be lonely, there's always someone . . . whose turn it is to be a helper."

"A real system."

"A tradition. Unofficial, of course. And very private."

"That's silly. I've never heard of that."

Susan raised her penciled eyebrows. "Suit yourself. But if a person wants in, all a person has to do is make contact."

"And I get some young-stuff captain in my bed."

"No, you get a major in your bed. Because your husband is a major."

Judy laughed. "What a crazy rumor!" She rolled from the hammock and straightened her shirt.

"Not too crazy. Ask Leona."

CHAPTER 5

Thursday, September 7, 1972

JUDY HAD INVITED this man into her bed. The only question now was: Would she go through with it? She had said no each of eighteen hundred nights. Surely she could be permitted one discreet infidelity, one affirmative answer to her young body. Was she to live like a nun?

His hands felt cool. They left little trails of bubbles where they touched her breast. There was no need to pretend. He had been frank about wanting her. It had nothing to do with love or respect. Afterward he would go away, and neither of them would speak of it again.

Ron would come home knowing what had intervened, but philosophy would win out. *You get through these things as best you can. War is hell.*

The man turned on his side now, pulling her over to him, pressing her against the length of his body. He had no macho physique—not exceptionally muscled or tall or demanding. But he was kind. Yes, she could say that. He acted like a partner in this lovemaking. She liked him very much. Ah, man. Man. How beautifully you are created. How thoroughly I need you.

"Mom?"

Lord, it was Kevin. She awoke, confused, tangled in the bedcovers. He would see. She sat up fearfully.

"It's after six-thirty, Ma. Did you set your alarm?"

The man had gone. She was alone. With flooding gratitude, she realized she had been dreaming.

"I guess I didn't. Okay." She lay back, still feeling the sexual warmth, trying to recall the man's face. Was it someone she knew? No. She didn't think so.

She reached over and switched on the bedside lamp. It came to her in a rush that she would never be able to think clearly if she didn't rearrange this bedroom. It was totally his—Ron's. She was like a mother whose child had died: Everything Ron had owned or even touched was in its place where he had left it. Time had ceased, the cracked-clock arrows stuck at 1967. Even his photograph had an old-fashioned look to it. The colors were paling. Something was draining the hues, minute by minute. And it wasn't even facing the sun.

Could Ron forgive her if she dared an infidelity? She studied the photo. A man of tremendous love, this man with the deep-set eyes and the dimpled chin; a man of American heartland parents and grandparents; a man thankful to be in the United States, proud to be a part of the Army. He was snow blond, and his smiling expression crinkled as though he were looking into a blinding dawn.

No. Her dream had only teased her. This man would not forgive. He cared with such intensity that there was no margin. Either one did, or one didn't. Amen.

She had loved him that way, too, with no second thoughts or sidelong glances to newcomers. But now she was neither wife nor widow. She was entombed.

If only the tomb were dim and silent. But it was built of flesh, and from it she could see and hear the joy of others.

Today she would put his books in the basement. She got up, decisively, and fingered the Chinese lettering on the bindings. How many texts were there on these floor-to-ceiling shelves? Two hundred? More? Why would a learned man like this have been risked in hostile territory? He was a political scientist and linguist, jobs which should have assured him noncombative status. But he spoke fluent Chinese. That was somehow the answer. The Army had need of him in Vietnam.

Judy envisioned herself carrying his books into the hall, starting heavily down the stairs. A peculiar flame lit the place behind her eyes. No! It would stir the pot, unsettle the forces of well-being, bring the wrath of his captors down on Ron. She felt dizzy.

Her frequent mood swings had lately begun to terrify

her. She viewed the divorce as the only haven: that neutral zone in which her feelings for Ron could no longer jeopardize him. Cutting the tie of matrimony would be like cutting the nerve endings of skin. The pathway would be dead. No more pain could travel to him. He would be safe from her fury and guilt.

Or would setting him adrift cause the ultimate harm, his death? He would know, without being told. His breath would be inexplicably sucked away from him through the slats of his bamboo cage.

I'm sick, she thought, looking into the bathroom mirror as she brushed her teeth. *Sick in the head.* This pronouncement did not cause her any discomfort, for she had read somewhere that the ones who can say they're crazy really aren't. She had made a ritual of acknowledging her mental instability at least once a day, usually in the morning.

"I didn't hear you come in last night," Leona said pointedly.

Judy, cracking four eggs into a pan, knew it was hopeless to bite on that. There was no response that could satisfy her mother-in-law.

Leona reached around Judy with a fork and began to stir the eggs into yellow clumps. Judy stepped aside and opened a bag of bread.

"I've already made biscuits."

"Oh. Thank you."

If only Leona would stay out of the way! It was impossible to prepare breakfast with her in the kitchen. She was always between Judy and something Judy wanted to get hold of. When Judy opened the refrigerator, Leona reached into it. When Judy turned on a faucet, Leona stuck a pan under the falling water.

It was no use to continue. Judy sat down at the table to watch Leona, a woman of wire. She had given birth six times, and Judy suspected she had enjoyed the exercise. Everything about her was no nonsense: the straight cut of her clothing; the way she held her head; the curlless home-cropped hairdo. Judy tried to picture Leona with makeup, but the vision was peculiar, clownish.

"You must have been having a great time." Leona, carrying the skillet, scraped eggs into three bowls on the table.

"I was."

She set the pan in the sink. There was a hiss and a bolt of steam. "What was the big event?" Leona would get it out of Judy or bust.

"Susan and I went to see *Patton* at the post theater." *Patton:* the story of the kingpin hawk. Judy had gone only to please Susan. Patton's zest for war made Judy's fingernails and teeth ache. But it was perversely fascinating, like an auto accident.

"Must have been a long one."

"Umm-humm."

Leona didn't fix food, she arranged it. The table bloomed with stewed apples, powder-puff muffins, pitchers of coffee and orange juice. A military widow, this proud lady, needing to be needed, turning her need into cakes and tall, perfectly layered parfaits; springing with energy that now was reflected only in household accomplishments. She shuttled between her far-flung children, state to state, on a precise schedule: four months with each child. Two years to make the complete tour. Her shelter was in whatever love they would share. It was an admirable and pitiful approach, Judy thought. Leona had arrived to stay with Judy on September 1 and would be gone the last day of December.

"Nugget was General Marshall's right hand, you know," Leona said, folding the napkins.

Judy did know. Her father-in-law's military record was exemplary. The Greer men had gunpowder in their blood. Military relatives could be documented back to the Revolutionary War. General Edward Greer had earned the nickname Nugget from Marshall, who considered him pure gold, a remarkable strategist. It was a terrible tradition to live under and live up to. Judy hoped Kevin would be a brain surgeon or a car salesman instead.

Judy gave a polite yes. Leona needed little prodding to trot out old stories of Nugget, stories of a time when winning or losing really mattered. How different Vietnam was from Hitler's Europe. It must have been so simple for Nugget.

"Marshall wrote to him until long after the war."

"Wrote to who?" Kevin appeared, yawning and looking hastily put-together.

"Your granddaddy." Leona smiled.

"Did what?"

"Knew a great general," Judy inserted, anxious to get it over with.

They sat around the table, heads bowed for a blessing. Judy had the beginnings of one on her lips, but Leona began earnestly: "Bless us, O Lord, and these thy gifts, which we are about to receive from thy bounty. Make us strong and able in your service. Make us humble and grateful. Lead us and guide us. In Jesus' name, amen."

Judy wondered if Leona truly felt led and guided. It was hard to imagine anyone leading or guiding Leona.

"*That woman* called last night," her mother-in-law said, passing the salt and pepper. Whenever Leona disapproved of someone, she did not call her by name. The outcasts were "that woman," "that man," "that girl" or "that boy."

"Who do you mean?"

"That woman from New York."

"Connie?"

Leona shrugged as though she couldn't remember.

"Was it Connie Roberts?"

"The peacenik."

Judy nodded, insulted. It was Connie.

"Am I to call her back?"

"She'll phone again."

Kevin was quietly packing away the kind of breakfast that twelve-year-olds eat. He had gone through several muffins and finished his eggs. The stewed apples were rapidly disappearing.

Judy examined him. A most appealing combination, this

child: Ron's corn-silk hair and her brown, pensive eyes. The shape of his face was narrow, like hers, but ended in Ron's prominently rugged chin. A soft sprouting of silvery fuzz dusted his upper lip, glistening now and then in the lamplight.

She adored the soul of this handsome son, but under the sleeve of his shirt she could perceive the throbbing of a permanent scar. The wound had recently faded from red to white with the façade of healing. Had she struck his heart, the effect would have been no less profound. There was a stranger now who inhabited Kevin's body at intervals, peering out, bewildered, from behind his eyes. When she reached down deep to embrace the little boy she had known, he drew back and avoided her overtures.

"Tell me about school," Judy said, touching the back of his hand and rubbing it lightly.

He thought. "Well . . ." Something pleasant passed before his gaze. "I won a race on Tuesday."

"You did? Why didn't you tell us before?" Judy felt a flush of happiness for him.

"I guess I just forgot."

"That's terrific. Who was racing?"

"The whole school. I won for the seventh grade."

"Well, I'm proud of you."

Leona nodded, smiling, chewing.

Kevin laid his fork onto his plate. "It was good, Leona."

Strange thing, a boy calling his grandmother by her first name. But Leona had always insisted on it. Judy decided this was a cross between Leona's public reason ("children should be treated as our equals") and the private reason: Leona desperately valued her youth. Muscle was everything. Her most abhorrent vision was that of someone helping her out of bed in the morning. The term "grandmother" had mystical powers. It could make the hair gray faster and perhaps contribute to its falling out. It could dry the ovaries up into raisins.

"Gotta go." Kevin pushed back the chair and leaned over to tie his sneakers.

Judy always felt at their parting that she should offer

Kevin something. To atone. And so she said, "Do you need any money?"

Kevin stood up and reached into his pocket, suddenly remembering the state of his finances. "I could use another five-spot."

"What did you do with the last one?" She smiled. "Eat it?"

"Literally." He picked up his books. "Lunch is up fifty cents this year."

"Okay then. Get it out of my purse in the hall."

Kevin put his hand on Judy's chair as he walked by. "So long."

"Bye, honey."

"Have a nice day," Leona called.

Her mother-in-law had never, in the four months since the shooting, mentioned it to Judy. It did not exist, could not have happened. It was kept in the mental file with ghosts and fairy tales. How would she deal with Judy's attempt at divorce? The thought made Judy wince.

Judy rose from the table and watched from the kitchen window as Kevin hefted his bookbag onto his back and rode down the driveway on his bicycle.

"Good breakfast, Leona." She helped clear the table and filled the sink with soapy water.

Leona, who already had her rubber gloves on, began to wash the egg-sticky plates vigorously. "I don't know why you want to keep on with that antiwar protesting," she said.

Judy knew this was the introduction to a monologue. She had been down this road before. "Now, Leona, this war isn't worth anything," she retorted. "They're not fighting to win over there. It's only a holding action. Containment. They should mop up or get out."

"We don't know what the government has in mind," Leona cautioned, setting the dripping plates into a drainer.

"We've been trusting all these years, and it hasn't helped Ron a bit."

"This kind of thing doesn't reflect well on Ron. You're

denying the very thing he stands for. People are watching you, too. Closely. It's not proper."

"The war's not proper. I need to get to work. It's almost time."

Leona finished her task with a thud of the faucet and a loud peeling of her rubber gloves. "Will you be home tonight?"

"Sure."

The two women eyed each other.

"Why don't you want me to go anywhere, Leona? Is it because you get lonely? Or is it because Ron can't go anywhere?"

Leona, surprised at the sudden honesty, allowed her mouth to slide from its usual half smile into a light grimace. She nodded in acknowledgment.

"Both?"

"Yes. I guess so."

"Well, I'm sorry." Judy, in a rush of tenderness for her husband's mother, put an arm around her shoulders. The shoulders tensed, hardened. Judy let go.

What was the message in Leona's face? It seemed to be a gratitude for Judy's reaching out to her. And yet Leona had pulled away. It wasn't Leona's style to be yielding. Not her style at all. Her love popped up in muffins and the cleaning of forgotten corners, in a hand towel fragrantly laundered and well placed on the bathroom vanity. Life for Leona couldn't be easy. She had come from a childhood of remote boarding schools into marriage with a man of determination and uncompromising ideals. Her actions had always been prescribed by others. Now she played the widow with an actor's dignity. People were watching. She must always meet their expectations.

There was apology in Leona's expression, but she remained rigid.

"See you tonight," Judy said, backing toward the door. She felt the calamity of aloneness wash over her again, stiffening her limbs, sending the hint of blackness to float beside her.

If only there were someone to hold her, joy flowing down the strength of his arms, feeding her. For so long now there had been no physical warmth, no acceptable means of tactile support. Everyone was off limits. Everyone was a potential threat to a decorum, to the proud pose she was expected to maintain as the wife of an official prisoner.

"All right." Leona's lips had curved again into the familiar pleased crescent.

Judy seemed, for a moment, to see Leona in parts: The good womb which had produced Ron, the lover of Judy's life, the most unusual and deserving person she had ever known. Leona's heart, which fled and hid, yet beat loyally for each soul bound to hers. The magnificent brain, which held at least twice as many memories as Judy's; which had in its private rooms visions of delight and death; which knew well the stark reality of *being there*. Unfathomable secrets. Languages. Vistas of crowded, peculiar countries. Mosques and scimitars and pampas grass. The lake ice and evergreens of Goose Bay, Labrador.

A most complete person: Leona. And yet strangely unsharing. The million mazes and mirrors of her mind turned in upon themselves, came to blind corners, reflected their own images over and over again.

Judy wanted to hold out an apron like a woman gathering apples and collect some of Leona's mysteries, use them to strengthen her own disintegrating life. But there was nothing Leona would let fall. Her ripeness fermented in a closed place.

Judy wondered whimsically if somewhere along the spongelike corridors of Leona's brain there was a rumor or perhaps a confirmation of Susan's sensual stories.

The thought of asking flittered once or twice in the space between Judy and Leona, then settled quietly to one side.

A memory. What if there were a memory in Leona of a sexual alliance during one of Nugget's many absences?

Impossible.

CHAPTER 6

JUDY WATCHED the aging two-story brick Colonial grow smaller and smaller in the rearview mirror. As always, she offered silent thanks that they could afford to rent it. Nothing could be more dismal, she thought, than to be relegated to one of the mistreated apartment buildings surrounding the post.

As her blue Dodge climbed the slight incline into Fort Harrison, she spent a second of thanks on the car, which was a miracle in itself. Ron had disappeared into Asian jungles, leaving all the Greers' worldly goods registered in his name alone. It was a legal quagmire to sell off anything, but with Tom's help she had finally ditched the Chevy and purchased a new car.

There were no gates or checkpoints, no guards at any entrance to Fort Harrison. Now, gliding along Fifty-sixth Street onto the post grounds, she became aware of its dollhouse quality. It was a village, tiny and perfect: something a child would find under the Christmas tree.

On the right were quarters for married enlisted personnel—frame town houses painted a cheerful avocado. On the left she could see the huge open park called the post green, a fairyland mall with a white summer gazebo and a cannon still in working order. Around the mall curved an avenue of forty-year-old brick duplexes behind the bright lace of slowly coloring leaves. These were the post's best homes, designated for senior officers.

Fort Ben was a gift used to reward retiring colonels for their years of service. It was the last, and finest, assignment: the home of those men and women affectionately dubbed the Remington Rangers—intellectuals who ran the Army not on its stomach but on its considerable brain. It included in its training centers Army, Navy, Air Force and Marine Corps standouts; many were enrolled at the Defense Department's Information School.

No scrap of paper, no bottle cap rested on the earth of Fort Harrison for more than a few hours. It was the Disneyland of military installations

She braked to a stop at an MP who was standing on a pedestal in the middle of the road, directing traffic. He pointed with precision—a picture from a recruiting magazine. Uniform perfectly pressed. Cap at just the right angle. Shoes glassy, white gloves dazzling in the morning glare. He motioned to her, and she turned into the long driveway of the Finance Center.

A monstrous building! Second in area only to the Pentagon. Its offices possessed a record of every payroll dollar spent on every Army man, woman or child anywhere in the world. Near its entrance, a garish self-important sign proclaimed: FINANCE CENTER, U.S. ARMY A ZERO DEFECTS COMMAND.

How she had become snared in this military net, she could no longer remember in detail. Repressed in her mental trove of days-gone-by was the Army's invitation to what it promised would be meaningful work.

She locked and slammed the car door, shivering in her brown wool cape. Her identification card, already pinned to her collar, received a nod from the guard.

The vast, impersonal empire of hallways and desks and files and telephones and overhead lights sucked her into its sadness, its sameness. She passed once again through the loneliest tunnel of her mind: the one that told her she, too, was a number. And that—worst of all—Ronald Greer was a number, an item as insignificant as corn and geese and locusts. She could see men, dying. Falling in the rice paddies, mud lining their open mouths. Could see their teeth, the white, gleaming American teeth that American mothers had brushed so patiently in the growing-up years. Dead teeth, the roots giving the final message to vibrant ceramiclike enamel: *Stop.*

And here ... in some room ... they paid all the mothers. Paid them off.

"Oh, no. Shit! Yaaaaa. Yike. Son of a bitch!"

Judy, on her way to the ladies' room, ran back quickly, snagged by masculine bellowing from the door she had just passed.

A uniformed man stood at a coffee urn. Its spout had fallen off, and hot coffee was pouring from the hole. He was futilely trying to catch the coffee in his cup, but black liquid had filled it and was overflowing onto the floor.

In the space of three seconds Judy considered carrying the urn to the sink, considered jamming the hole with a wad of napkins, considered pushing the man back out of the line of fire. He obviously had lost the ability to reason and was scalding his hand.

She reached for a metal wastebasket and shoved it under the gushing stream. He dropped his cup into the basket and jumped around, shaking his burned hand, making angry noises from behind pressed lips.

As the coffee drained into the wastebasket and slowed to rapid drops, the man fished a handkerchief out of his pocket and wrapped it around his fingers. Judy looked up into his face. He was grinning. Dare she grin back? Now he let go with a tremendous belly laugh, and she, releasing all her tension, laughed heartily.

He was a major. Gold leaves twinkled on his epaulets. But she didn't recognize him. Not unusual. People came and went with regularity. Fort Ben was a parade of faces.

They stared at the wastebasket, which by now was a bucket of coffee, nearly full.

"It's a forty-cup wastebasket, wouldn't you say?" He laughed again.

She smiled. "How did this happen?"

"Just lucky, I guess."

Judy glanced up at him. *A nice person. You can always tell.* Clean hair; curly, dark. Green eyes. Extra-heavy eyebrows. He had a happiness in his manner that startled her. She understood from the lines that fanned out at his eyes and cut lightly next to his mouth that he was used to pleasure, not grief.

"Joe Campbell," he said, introducing himself.

"Judy Greer. You're new?"

"Fairly. Came in a couple weeks ago."

"I hadn't seen you before."

"It's a big place. Right?"

She regarded the wastebasket full of coffee.

"I'll pour it out," he offered. "Thanks for helping me."

"Sure. Bye now."

"So long. Thanks again." He was already hefting the wastebasket.

"I told him we didn't need all that stuff." Susan plunked her tray onto Judy's table at the post cafeteria and started unloading it.

Judy, who was halfway through her Jell-O salad, waited. It was Susan's habit to begin a conversation in the middle, and Judy knew she would soon be informed as to who didn't need what.

Susan's lunch was a smorgasbord of chicken, rice, peas, cherry pie, applesauce, tea and rolls. She always had her big meal at noon, complaining she had no one to cook for anymore. Now she slid her empty tray onto a neighboring table and sat down, pulling her chair up with a scraping noise. "We don't need it; why should we get it? But *no*, he says." She slammed a sugar pack onto the table several times to shake the granules to one end and ripped it open, ceremoniously dumping the white powder into her iced tea. She did the same with a second pack and a third, then stirred the whole thing vigorously.

"We keep getting these stupid supplies we don't need. Can you believe it?"

Judy could.

"I go down there every month, and I spend the damned allotment; then I can hardly get all those note pads and pens and ledgers and whatever else into our cupboard. And it all has to be locked up." She cut into the chicken breast. "If I put one more paper clip in there, the whole cabinet will explode." Susan finally glanced at Judy for the first time since her arrival. "What's the smile?"

"Why not?"

"Come on now, Judy, you know you only smile every other Tuesday."

Judy took a bite of her sandwich.

"Allotments being what they are," Susan continued, "we can't get less because next month we might need more, and then they'll say—"

"You didn't spend sixty dollars last month, so we cut your allotment back to forty-five, the amount you *did* spend."

"Yeah. Isn't that the nuttiest system?"

Judy nodded. The allotment system was notorious. Still, Susan must be exaggerating. You wouldn't just go on month after month getting supplies you knew wouldn't be used. Susan was given to hyperbole. It was one of her charms.

"Who's Campbell?" Judy said, chewing her tuna fish.

"How'd you meet *him*?"

Susan, of course, would know Campbell even if he'd only been on post a few hours. She had networks of friends and missed nothing. She was a human information-retrieval system, loaded with fact and myth. The trick was to be sure which was which.

"He had an accident with a coffee urn. The spout came off and fell in his cup." It amused her to remember his humor in the face of humiliation.

"He's new," Susan said, attacking the rice.

"What division?"

"Oh, all around. He's some kind of adviser out of Washington. I don't know ... might be some kind of efficiency expert. Better type faster."

Judy finished her dill pickle. "They're not going to fire me this year."

"You think so?" Susan played along.

"Not this year. They've already used up their allotment of typists. Can't get any more till next year."

Susan winked and rubbed her nose with a napkin.

Judy left work in a light rain, covering her hair with the brown cape. Luckily the Dodge wasn't too far away. She started across the lot. It was well past four, and most of the others had gone. The pedestaled MP was nowhere in sight.

She had the feeling of someone just behind her and turned suddenly, colliding with a major's uniform.

"Oh, I'm sorry." Barnes. She knew him from Bink's going-away party. He worked in the bowels of the Finance Center.

"My fault." He lingered as if contemplating a speech.

"How are you, Paul?"

"Very well."

"That's good. See you later."

"Judy?"

"Yes?"

"I'll . . . walk you to your car."

What the . . . ? "Okay."

He fell into step beside her, the rain making dark dots all over his cap. She opened the door and got in. He leaned forward to speak with her. He was younger than most majors and kept his hair quite short . . . golden and bristly.

"How are you getting along?"

"Fine."

"Is there anything that I . . . could do for you?"

Their eyes connected, and understanding clicked into place. She became incensed.

"No," she said, turning her key and starting the car. She put her hand on the door to close it. He held it open.

"Judy . . . I . . ."

She wanted to be sure. She looked fully into his gaze. The tender, hairless face with no hint of beard. The brown eyes with speckles of amber. No mistake.

"I mean . . ."

"I think I know what you mean."

"I would be willing to do anything to help you," he said sincerely. "Yours is a very difficult situation."

She pulled harder on the door. He wedged his elbow in it.

"Look. I would keep your confidence. Whatever you

need, well . . . that would be just between us."

She felt the heat of anger curling through her chest. "Did Susan send you?"

He blanched, then colored pink in splotches across his face and neck. "Judy, forgive me. I was only trying to help."

"No, thanks."

He released his grip on the door, and she closed it. She smacked the lock down with her fist and jammed the car into reverse. He stood there in the rain, saying something, motioning to her with apology as she turned the car in a small space and pulled out of the driveway. Her fingers were perspiring with rage, slipping along the steering wheel. She wiped them one by one on her cape.

In the commissary Judy hesitated over every item. If only there weren't so many brands of each thing. She paused between the stacks of cans and boxes for several minutes at a time, scuffing her feet on the wooden floor, trying to decide. Kellogg's. Del Monte. Libby's. When at last she put each box of cereal or can of peaches into the cart, she experienced a second of regret. Was it the right choice? *No,* she chided herself. *It doesn't matter. It doesn't really matter.*

She threw things into the cart with a little more determination now, ending at the meat counter. The bloody redness made her uncomfortable.

In line, waiting to pay, Judy saw Kevin's homeroom teacher checking out with half a dozen loaves of bread and three gallons of milk. Mrs. Hanover had a lot of children. She suddenly reflected pity when she recognized Judy. Her wide, powdered cheeks, plump like pastry, crumpled in concern as her jaw drooped and a frown overtook her.

"How are you, Mrs. Greer?"

"Just fine." Judy forced a smile and wished they'd hurry packing her things into the bag.

"Kevin's doing well."

"That's good." Judy nodded. Mrs. Hanover had been

Kevin's teacher for only a few days, but she was legendary for her savvy and discipline. Judy had hoped Kevin would get her this year, but she wanted Mrs. Hanover to take the pity out of her voice.

As they walked together through the parking lot, Judy thought of Kevin's race. That was something to break the ice, to make things a little more normal.

"I heard about the race," Judy said, hoping for a description of Kevin's agility.

"Yes, it was a lot of fun. We were sorry Kevin didn't want to participate this year."

"He didn't?"

"Why, no." Mrs. Hanover stopped rolling her laden shopping cart. "He just . . . didn't want to. But it was all right. No one has to run. Some children don't enjoy the competition. It's all right." She was obviously reading Judy's stricken eyes.

"Sometimes," Mrs. Hanover said sympathetically, "it's not to the child's advantage to compete." She pushed her cart the few remaining feet to her car and opened the trunk. "Don't worry about it."

Kevin had lied.

"Oh, I wanted to ask you . . ." Judy began.

Mrs. Hanover flashed her full attention at Judy. A beacon. Kindness. "Yes?"

"Is the school lunch more expensive this year?"

"No." She seemed pleased to give the answer Judy wanted. "They finally held the line on it. Can you believe?"

When Judy entered the kitchen, Kevin was studying at the table and the phone was ringing. Didn't he hear it? She stumbled across the room in a rush, set the grocery sack on the floor and picked up the receiver. "Hello?"

Kevin looked up.

"Mrs. Greer?" A young boy.

"Yes?"

"Is Kevin there?"

"Yes."

"Will you tell him we're waiting for him? Coach is really mad."

"Just a minute, please. Kevin." She held the phone out to him. He knew. She could see that. He took his time getting to her.

"Yeah?" He listened.

Judy started to shove cornflakes and napkins onto shelves.

"Yah," Kevin was saying. "Okay, okay. I guess I forgot. Right." He hung up, glanced guiltily at her.

"Well?"

"I guess I missed practice."

"Is it still going on?"

"Yes."

"I'll drive you down there."

"Ah, Mom . . . I have this report to do for school." He motioned toward the books.

"You told me you didn't have practice today."

"Oh." He shuffled over to the table and sat down again. "I have this report to do."

"So you decided to skip."

He shrugged.

"That's not fair, Kevin. If you're going to be on the team, you're supposed to show up for all the practices."

He held a book up to his face and started reading it.

"Wait a minute now." She walked over and touched the book, pressing it lightly onto the tabletop. "Kevin . . ." She leaned down to be on eye level.

"I forgot, Mom. Okay?"

"Let's get in the car right now and go down there."

He reluctantly closed the book.

"Kevin," she said gently, "I talked to Mrs. Hanover today . . . about the race."

He flinched.

"And the lunch money."

"Now, look, I'll be right here in an hour to pick you up."

Kevin nodded and got out of the car. She watched him

walk toward the jumble of young men assembled on the City League ball field. One was taller than all the others. She squinted. Must be the coach. Looked like ... that Campbell guy! How could that be? Gene Crimmins had been running the team last she knew.

The huddle broke up, and each player took a position. The ball was snapped back, and uniforms scattered everywhere.

Uncanny that Campbell would turn up twice in one day.

CHAPTER 7

Monday, September 11, 1972

KEVIN COULDN'T sleep. Through the hardwood floor came the angry voices of his mother and his grandmother, arguing in the living room.

"If you think I'm going to stay here and be your baby-sitter while you go to Washington on that foolishness . . ." Leona scolded.

"There may be some prisoners coming out of Hanoi," his mother retorted, "a direct result of the antiwar effort. *They're* doing it. And Kissinger isn't. I'm going to be there."

"It's a lot of hooey," Leona said, exasperated. "Why can't you work within the system? Why can't you let the government handle it?"

"Because the government's *not* handling it. And people like Ron are dying because of the waiting, waiting, waiting. They're putting us on, Leona—the whole bunch of them."

"But why do *you* have to get involved?"

"Ron is dying," she said again, her words edged with fear.

He heard Leona's distinct footfall, stomping on the stairs, heard her shut the door to her room. After a few minutes his mother came up, too, and all was quiet.

He crept to the living room and huddled in a corner of the sofa, rubbing his bad arm. There were hurtful things in this place: feelings like knives, still flying from the walls. He sat in the darkness for a long time.

In his make-believe, he emerged from a stand of fern and walked on cat feet next to the buildings of Hanoi. The dusty streets were deserted and beginning to throw shadows in his path. He knew his father by the sound of his breathing, and he followed that thin, rattling whine to a cell. It was bamboo, about eight feet by eight feet—with standing water on the dirt floor, a wooden pail and nothing else but his feverish father, hunkering in a corner.

Kevin whispered to him, and his father looked up, amazement and hope registering in the flat, windowlike eyes. His father didn't know him, of course, for he had grown. But he seemed to recognize the shape of his son's head and the blond Nordic hair.

There were no locks on the cage, just a small wooden post wedged into a couple of hemp loops. Very simple, really. But impossible to reach from the inside; the bars were too close together.

Kevin pushed the post with his thumb, and it fell, tapping, onto the ground. And now he was reaching for his father: a stick figure with no flesh left for Kevin to embrace. He would fatten him with whipped cream. Pancakes. Candy bars. And then there would be a lap for crawling up on, and muscles for gripping the boy tightly about the shoulders.

His father couldn't walk, so Kevin carried him like a baby. Will born of triumph and horror kept him from exhaustion.

They saw no one; no evil barred their path. The dewy fern splashed their foreheads as they traveled smoothly into the enfolding jungle.

Kevin lay back against the sofa cushions. If only his father were dead, Kevin could relinquish the haunting image of rescue. He was weary from playing the same scene over and over. Sometimes his father could walk, sometimes the cage was guarded by a snake that Kevin had to kill, but the basic mission remained the same. For Kevin to act it out and act it out again had become a ritual to take the place of prayer. Where prayer had failed, the rehearsal for rescue succeeded.

As long as rescue was being enacted somewhere in someone's mental power, it was still a possibility. To abandon the ritual would be to abandon his father, and Kevin knew that he, as the only son, was his father's single hope.

He squeezed tears from beneath his eyelids and let them flow over his face. It was part of the whole thing—the last part: the ultimate communication, a way of feeding to his father a lifeline of emotion. A way of caressing him. Of making him understand that he was missed.

"Kevin?" His mother had come quietly into the room. She must have caught the glitter of tears in the moonlight, for she sat in the rocker and patted her knees. Could she mean for him to come to her? He got up. This was silly. He was nearly as big as she. She smiled at him, holding out her arms, and he lowered himself gingerly onto her lap.

"Kevin?" His mother's voice, from the stairs. He leaped from the rocker. "Are you all right?" She was leaning over the banister, trying to see him through the darkness.

"Yes."

She descended a step or two. "Come on to bed now, okay?"

He looked at the rocker. It was still swaying back and forth with their weight.

Tuesday, September 12, 1972

KEVIN'S HEAD began to perspire under his helmet. The drops trickled into his eyes, so that he had to keep rubbing them. He had, so far, caught a knee in the stomach and a set of cleats on the hand. These bastards were out to get him.

He glanced around the field at the dozen and a half boys who were taking a break from practice and limbering up in various ways. Under their football shirts the padding shifted in lumps. He was a better player than most of them. He knew that. But they were determined to kill him, get him off the team. He spit into the grass.

He didn't fit here. He didn't fit in anywhere. They wanted to stamp the life out of him. It had something to do with his father. A prisoner. A source of shame. . . . Or his mother and her marches.

He took the field at Coach Campbell's wave of an arm, lining up with the others for scrimmage. The ball went into play. He started to run, covering his man.

With a slash of crimson, an elbow slammed into his face guard, jarring his cheekbones and bringing a toothy taste of blood. As he tried to dodge another player who had come up behind him on his left, he felt a helmet butt into the small of his back. He fell, with a grinding pain, rolling back and forth to relieve the agony. No one offered him a hand.

He staggered to his feet. The eyes behind the face guards were tentative, calculating.

He wasn't stupid. He knew it was because he was different, like the way the kids had tried to get Gordon Whitesell in the second grade. Poor Gordie with the funny little hand hanging on half an arm.

The players squared off again at the line. Now the ball hopped into the air: a brown, grainy oval glinting in the September afternoon warmth. Andy Warner drew his hand back and let the ball sail; Justin Helms caught it. Kevin barreled down the field in pursuit of the quarterback.

God! He crashed to his knees. Someone had thrown his entire weight across the calves of Kevin's legs. He bit his upper lip to keep from crying out. A vision of Tom Wellington passed in front of him. A memory. They had been eating at an Indianapolis lunch counter, a high school hangout, just catching a fast sandwich, talking. Wellington was in uniform, a red flag in front of twenty bulls. One by one, the students came by and taunted him, cruising close to him, brushing against his back, spilling his Coke. Finally, they grabbed his cap from the counter and tossed it back and forth. In the second it took Tom to turn and stand up, the cap had vanished. They found it later in the men's room toilet. Vietnam was the bucket of shit everybody wanted to kick—especially kids his age. A military uniform was a pleasant target.

Judy arrived early to pick up Kevin. Sighing leaves

skittered this way and that as they rained down from dozens of maples. She could see the boys pulled together in two huddles, but she was too far away to spot Kevin except by his number, 36.

Judy held back a little, knowing that mothers were taboo at practice. Her early appearance would throw the whole thing off, and Kevin would come home brooding.

Instead of standing on the sidewalk, she half hid behind a parked car, rested her chin on her hands and watched as the practice continued. She was glad Kevin had wanted to play football. It was one of the few things he still participated in. And he was good. His size and weight were just average; but he had a bearlike way of charging his opponents, and a lot of them opted to get out of the way.

She had been gazing passively at the action, but now she moved toward the group with compelling curiosity. It wasn't only the ballcarrier who was being pursued. It seemed that people were chasing . . . Kevin! What a peculiar notion. She got as close as she dared, not wanting anyone to spot her. They were still at quite a distance, and she hurried between trees with anxious stealth.

Kevin fell heavily. An audible crack reached her a second later. What had she heard? His leg? She watched with growing anger as he got up shakily and resumed play, only to be crushed in a sadistic sideways body tackle.

If Kevin brought down the carrier, everyone piled on him, jumping with their full weight. If he ran to one side, there would be four or five bodies after his. On the third-down play a boy smashed Kevin in the throat with his forearm.

Where's the coach?

Even as she thought it, Campbell stepped forward, strode into the crowd and spoke sharply. They all turned toward him. He motioned for a conference. The boys sauntered from various parts of the field, hands on their hips, heads held in defiant poses. She couldn't hear what he said, but she could make out the set of his chin. He was furious, gesturing with his fists and dispersing the players with an irate wave. They took off their helmets and tucked them under their arms, slouched away, not looking back. Kevin alone stayed, pacing, saying something belligerent to Campbell, pointing at him.

Campbell must have called them on what they were doing to Kevin, and Kevin was embarrassed to be singled out. He'd want to handle his own trouble.

Campbell and Kevin faced each other now. Surely Kevin wouldn't get into it with the coach.

Kevin lowered his helmeted head and ran at Campbell, aiming for his abdomen. Campbell stepped aside and Kevin missed.

Pivoting quickly, Kevin tried again. This time he caught Campbell in the ribs. But Campbell was powerful, and Kevin much smaller. She could tell that Campbell was unaffected by the blow. Again and again, Kevin came at the man, smacking into him with the top of his helmet. She was frozen, appalled. But Campbell seemed undisturbed, holding Kevin off easily with hands to Kevin's shoulders, moving with him, accepting his fury.

Judy began to run toward them. All the youngsters had disappeared now, gone to their homes. There was no one in sight but these two opponents so strangely doing battle. When she was still twenty yards away, she heard Kevin break into an anguished sob. He stopped hurling himself at Campbell and knelt at his feet, reaching up to him, grasping at him. With visible compassion, Joe Campbell stooped down to put his arms around Kevin, his tenderness deliberate, unhurried. Embraced him.

Campbell glanced up, then, and saw her where she had stopped midway down a leafy embankment. He motioned gently for her to go back. To go away.

CHAPTER 8

Friday, September 15, 1972

"JUDY!" SUSAN drew her out of the September night and into the cartwheels of music. Susan's living room and den seethed with bodies undulating to the deafening beat, lounging against walls, smoking, drinking, sitting on the couch, lying on the floor, quarreling and flirting next to a well-stocked bar. Someone had opened the French doors at the other side of the den, and their white chiffon curtains puffed and waved like truce flags.

The uniforms were all colors, all ranks. Susan never limited her parties to officers. Any lively being was welcome. Susan digested parties like food; they sustained her through the long days of Bink's Korea stint.

"Come on, Judy, I've got lots of people for you to meet."

No place to hide. Why was she here? She gave serious thought to going home. No, she couldn't hurt Susan. She had accepted this invitation because she had rejected so many other overtures from Susan. She didn't want to destroy the friendship.

Susan took her arm and squeezed it, leaned her head close to Judy's. "There are lots of fantastic people here. Keep an open mind."

Judy's eyes lit on Barnes, who was coming in through the French doors. She hesitated. "Susan . . ."

Susan was also noticing Barnes, who went directly to the fireplace and prodded the glowing logs with a poker.

"Why did you do that to me?"

"What?"

"Send that . . . Barnes . . . to proposition me. I don't need that."

"He did?"

Judy studied Susan's lips, which were slightly parted in surprise.

"Don't ever do that again."

"But I . . ." Susan started to protest. "Okay, okay. I'm sure he takes no for an answer. You don't have to be afraid to come in."

Afraid. That word sent Judy's blood pressure up a few points. She certainly wasn't afraid of anybody like baby-face Barnes.

Susan drew Judy over to the bar. "What'll you have?"

"Just a . . ."

"Live it up!" Susan exclaimed, holding her arms out wide. "Come on, girl! I'll make you a delight, but don't look."

"All right." Judy leaned against the bar and scanned the room. Behind her, Susan dropped ice cubes into a blender. Judy could hear the *clank-clink,* and the noisy grinding when she pushed the button.

"There now." Susan poured the concoction into a tall glass. "It's going to be delicious." She stuck a pineapple chunk and a cherry on a swizzle stick and stabbed it into Judy's drink. The liquid was pale yellow and frothy.

"What is this?"

"See if you can guess." She shoved it into Judy's hand. "I've got to go patrol the bedrooms. People are always getting into the beds. As a good house mother I can't have *that* going on." She wrinkled her nose and swished around the side of the bar toward the hallway.

Judy did not want to be left alone in this mass of faces. She found a quiet corner and sat gingerly into a beanbag chair, taking a suspicious sniff of her drink. Nothing potent, she guessed. Okay to sip. Um, sweet. The coldness numbed her tongue.

She was just beginning to feel a slight kick from the alcohol when she noticed Joe Campbell standing at the other end of the room, talking to three men. He had his back to her. No mistaking the confident posture and animated gestures, though. He was telling something humorous, and the men were following it with glee. As the bunch disbanded, Campbell headed for the bar and spotted Judy. He came to her with an affectionate smile. Through the shared scene with Kevin, they were no longer strangers. Apprehension touched her.

He knelt on the floor beside the listing beanbag chair. "You're going to fall out of that thing." He pushed at it a little. "Here. Let me see if I can keep you from being lopsided."

She grinned. "Have you ravished any more coffee urns lately?"

"Three or four." He laughed.

"Shame on you."

Thoughts of Kevin floated thickly between them. They sobered.

"I'm worried about your son," he said. "There's something very wrong."

"Yes."

"Is there some way I can help?"

"I doubt it. Just . . . what you've done." It embarrassed her to think of Kevin's open hostility and Campbell's willingness to meet it. "You don't have to get involved."

"You're right. I'm stepping on toes." He went to get up.

"Wait . . ." But he was already on his feet. "Major Campbell . . " She tried to get out of the beanbag chair, without success.

Campbell put a hand under her arm and pulled her to a standing position. "Joe."

"I didn't mean to insult you."

"You're not insulting me. You're right. It's between you and Kevin. It's a sticky situation. I can appreciate that." He was still holding her arm, and warmth was creeping to her shoulder and down toward her elbow.

A flush inched across her cheeks. He let go.

"Judy! I want you to meet Ned Dowling." Susan. Out of nowhere. "Ned, this is my good friend, Judy Greer, and . . ." She paused, looking at the spot on Joe's chest where his name tag would have been, but he was wearing his civvies.

"Joe Campbell," he said, shaking Ned's hand.

"Ned's just back from Nam. We've got to give him lots of TLC."

Ned grunted and took a swig of his beer. His freckles began in his orange hair and covered every square inch of skin that she could see. The pinkness of his complexion had been deepened by the evening's alcohol.

Susan grabbed Judy's drink and held a new one out to her. She took it reluctantly.

"Not good?" Susan said with mock offense.

"It's good, but I don't want to overdo it."

"Overdo it," Ned snorted, taking another gulp.

Campbell, who seemed to be put off by Ned, mumbled, "Excuse me," and walked away.

"So, what were you doing in Nam?" Judy asked, trying to make conversation.

"Don't ask."

"Oh." *That was my one effort,* she decided. *Let him think of something to talk to me about.*

"Dog tags," he said.

"What?"

"Dog tags. You know. End of the line. The last depot. Dog tags."

"Do you mean the dead soldiers?"

"Yeah. Them."

Now she was intently reading his blue eyes. These eyes had seen Vietnam's American dead.

"You mean you had something to do with . . . sending them home?"

"Yep. Rack 'em, stack 'em."

Judy recoiled.

"I didn't work on the bodies, no. I made the packages."

Whatever was he talking about? Judy looked for Susan, but she was not in sight.

Noticing her baffled frown, he said, "Personal effects. You gotta make sure nothing gets home in those cartons that could wipe out a family, ya know?"

"Like what?"

"Awww . . . old love letters to Ying Yong or Saigon Susie, you get me?"

"Yes."

"Aaaand . . . and rubbers. They're not s'pposed to have no rubbers. Who're they fuckin'? Their wife's at home, ya see?"

Distaste for Ned began to dilate Judy's veins.

"And drugs. You know. You don't want to think your son's no hophead. Or your husband. You gotta get rid of that shit. You don't send it home."

"I see." How polite of the Army. How thoughtful. They wouldn't want to send anything obscene home. Mercy, no. Just the ripped-up, bullet-riddled, gut-spewing body hardening with time.

"Pardon me." Judy headed for Susan, who had appeared behind the bar.

"Is that guy on the level?"

"Who?"

Judy gestured toward Ned, who was picking at his specialist stripes and belching with an open mouth.

"I doubt it. Why?"

"He said his time in Nam was spent sending care packages to parents."

"Oh, yeah," Susan acknowledged. "He told me that."

"Is it true?"

"Who knows? Does it matter?"

"It might."

"Hey, now, cheer up. The guy's a ding-a-ling."

"He said he cleaned out things like love letters and condoms and drugs."

"Drugs I could vouch for. Ned made a million dollars selling drugs in Nam."

Judy gave Susan a skeptical look.

"Half a million then. I have it on good authority." Pause. "A quarter of a million? Maybe a hundred thousand?"

Judy giggled in spite of herself. "Susan, you're the limit."

"He did, Judy! Now I know where he got all that junk."

Unfortunately Carolyn Vincent showed up. Judy had been avoiding her. Carolyn was the head of Waiting Wives.

"Where have you been?" She materialized in front of Judy, wearing a gold-trimmed white pantsuit over a svelte figure. No wrinkle, no mist of perspiration ever showed up on Carolyn. She waited neatly and placidly for her husband's return. Her days were powdered, and trimmed with expensive—but never large—jewelry. "I haven't seen you for a long time. We've missed you at the meeting. How have you been?"

"Fine."

"I wish you'd come back. Everybody's asked about you."

She regarded Carolyn's coiffure, arranged hair by hair; the careful makeup of her features, lipstick, rouge, not too much, just enough. And under it all, a perceptible soft-ness. Sincerity. Yes, in spite of the ornaments, that's what she had . . . heart, at the very center.

She's a good person, Judy thought with a tremor of con-science. But Judy's outspoken views on Vietnam had spread a chill through the group. Many of their husbands were fighting in that war. Only a few people like Carolyn still radiated cordiality.

"Won't you come back?" Carolyn asked with no trace of judgment in her voice.

"I can't."

These women all had letters from their husbands. The pulse was steady, though faint. Judy had never had a letter from Ron, although she and Kevin and Leona had written nearly a thousand. Her only assurance that Ron existed as a prisoner of war was the insistence of the State Depart-ment. He had been seen in a Hanoi prison camp.

In the Christmas films that were delivered out of North Vietnam, she had never glimpsed his face. Once or twice the paranoid thought occurred to her that the govern-ment had clipped him out as a punishment for her peace efforts, left the frame-by-frame story of his waning life on some cutting-room floor. And the letters from him? Well, perhaps there had never been any. Perhaps they had been

intercepted by the Communists long before they reached
U.S. zones.

And the letters she had written? She could picture the
Vietcong using them for latrine paper.

She and Joe Campbell had stalked each other most of
the evening. A cord of curiosity was tied between them,
and every now and then it gave a good yank—which Judy
tried to ignore.

Finally, he came and sat beside her on the sofa.

"So, what's up?" he shouted close to her temple. The
music had grown steadily louder as the party progressed.

Judy's arms and legs consisted of warm liquid. She had
drunk four of Susan's "delights."

"With me?" she shouted back.

"Yes! What's happening next?" He gestured impatiently
for her to follow him onto the back porch.

"That's better," he said in a normal tone as the music
jumped and drifted behind them. "I think I can actually
hear your answer now, although my cochlea is somewhat
traumatized."

She shot him an amused glance.

"My cochlea." He pointed to the side of his head. "It's
the inner part of your ear."

They both laughed.

"So what's your answer?"

"I'm going away for a couple of days."

"Vacation?"

"Washington. They're bringing three POWs home."

"Yours?"

"No. I'm going to support the antiwar activists."

He nodded somberly.

"You don't approve?" Here it was again. She couldn't
mesh with anyone, even for a few minutes. Because they
didn't understand. They didn't use the mind's eye to look
down on Vietnam, to see the beautiful village children try
to outrun the napalm burning into their backs, see the
torrential water from bombed dams sweep away life-giv-

ing rice. They didn't see the disoriented GI's night-black-ened view from a plane, see him pushed out the door at a precise and counted interval, see him jerked suddenly by the D ring, parachuting into machine-gun fire. Where was the enemy? Who was? Which way to go? Shoot at what?

Fight to win? Take? No. Contain, contain. But how? *How,* when there was no definite shape of helmet to aim at, when death could be brought by an old lady carrying a grenade in a baby blanket.

Survival. The only thing. Just to stay alive. To get home again. The hell with it.

"Never mind," she said angrily, backing away from him.

"Hey . . ." He caught her by the shoulder.

"Don't . . ." Judy pushed his hand. He released her. They stood eyeing each other.

"I want to know," he whispered.

"Want to know what?"

"How you feel. The truth. The way you see it."

"It would take forever to tell, and I haven't got time." Fury was shaking her stomach. The words came out in loud, halting pieces.

"Why?"

"Because people . . . are dying. Every minute I waste, people are dying. For nothing. And you! Are part of it! Major!"

He drew his chin in a little, as if taking a blow, but his expression didn't change. It was still accepting, open to her. Wasn't there anything she could say that would make him fight back? This was the way he had handled Kevin. A strange man. An unusual man.

"Tell me. Make me see what you see."

"Not now. Sometime. Maybe."

He shifted ever so slightly closer to her, and she became aware of the heat he was giving off into the clear, cold evening. She thought she could feel it curling through the countless tiny holes of her sweater knit, sliding chamber by chamber onto her flesh.

CHAPTER 9

Friday, September 22, 1972

JUDY AND LEONA pounded each other on the shoulders. Around them, people of all ages, bundled in thick clothing, yelled and flailed their arms under the glaring lights of the City League Field. Kevin's team had won its first game of the season. The lead had changed hands six times, and most spectators had left their seats to press against the barrier rope which encircled the field. Now chaos reigned: cheers and the shuffling of bodies; young people running in all directions.

In the opposing stands the departure of fans was orderly, quiet. Judy had expected to be mournful, too, but it was a Cinderella evening. She could see Kevin smiling under his helmet, making his way toward her. He waved. The team had played in harmony with him. It may have been a grudging harmony, but he had traveled the field without mishap and been a key participant in two crucial plays.

He motioned for her to come down to where he was. She put her arm through Leona's and helped her step from bench to bench across the bleachers. Such a simple moment to bring so much pleasure! The comfortable locking of elbows with her mother-in-law, Kevin's flushed look of exultation.

They had almost reached him now but were being buffeted by people in a hurry. The pace quickened, families rushing to speak with their victorious sons. Judy and Leona met Kevin at the rope.

"Congratulations, honey!" Judy exclaimed, and Leona reached out to grasp Kevin's hand. He nodded in acknowledgment.

"Coach wants to bring pizzas to our house."

Startled, Judy looked at Campbell, who was gathering equipment at the other side of the field. People galloped by at intervals to poke his arm and offer praise.

"Can he, Mom?"

"Well, I don't understand. What do you mean?"

"We wanna have a team party, and Coach offered to buy all the pizzas; but we need a place. Can they come, Mom? Can they come to our house?"

It occurred to Judy that Kevin had not asked for anything in a very long time. It was embarrassing, sad, that she hadn't noticed it until now.

"Sure."

"Yippee!" He leaped and flung his hands out wide, then ran away into a tangle of red shirts and helmets.

But would they accept his invitation? Would they show up?

When she opened the door, she recognized Joe Campbell's eyes grinning over a stack of pizza boxes. Behind him was—it must be—the entire team. And girl friends! Shy, softly rounded faces; long, straight hair. Girls! She hadn't realized Kevin was old enough. She had seldom seen him with his peer group, *Her fault.*

"Hello! Come on in!" She stepped back, and Campbell carried the pizzas to the kitchen, the children streaming in behind him with potato chips, dip, cartons of cola, paper plates and cups. They were eager and attractive—the boys speaking in voices alternately deep and shrill; the girls bright with anticipation, their figures lean and lightly budding.

"Thank you for inviting us," the last one in said as Judy closed the door.

Leona descended the stairs. Judy knew she had been washing the bathroom sink. To Leona, even a sprinkling of toothpaste on the hardware or a hint of soap film at the drain would be cause for uneasiness. Leona smiled, staring at all the boys and girls who had flocked to the living room and begun lithe, easy dancing.

"Lady Willpower, it's now or never, give your love to me," the man on the record sang with demanding cadence. "Lady Willpower . . ."

Judy moved to the kitchen. Campbell was dealing pizza slices onto an array of paper plates. He gave her a friendly glance, then noticed Leona.

"You must be Mrs. Greer. I'm glad to know you. I'm Joe Campbell."

"How do you do." Leona regarded him with curiosity and admiration.

Joe pulled paper cups from a stack and stood them in rows. "I forgot the ice," he said sheepishly.

"Oh, well . . . I have ice." Judy opened the refrigerator and pulled the bin out of the freezer compartment. "Here."

He took it. "I wanted to have a victory party but couldn't think of a good spot. Kevin was nice enough to say he'd ask you. I hope it's all right."

"Of course."

She and Leona began setting full plates and cups on the dining room table. The children snapped them up. "Thank you," they murmured. "Thank you, thank you."

Judy looked at each boy closely. Could these be the angry souls who had beset Kevin? They had changed their minds—at least temporarily. She thought she knew why. Joe Campbell.

Now she watched him walk through the group, radiating magnetism. He squeezed elbows and shook hands. He turned the lamps up to their brightest setting, opened windows. His generous laughter rose above the music. It almost seemed she was in someone else's house—no longer agonizingly responsible minute by minute. Someone else was steering. The place of endless waiting and of daily routine stirred with unexpected excitement.

Campbell clowned a little and then bowed out of the action. He had even brought his own trash bags and set about cleaning up the kitchen.

"I thought you were going to Washington," he said as

they poured leftover cola out of paper cups and dumped pizza crusts.

"Soon. The POWs are due to board the plane in Vietnam tomorrow."

"I read about it: 'released to the custody of antiwar activists.' That's what you were talking about, wasn't it?"

"Yes. But it's New York instead of Washington."

"Well, don't forget to come back," he said, tying up the last plastic bag with a flourish. "We're having a canoe trip next weekend for the team and their parents. I hope we'll see you." He leaned against the counter, waiting for her answer.

Why was he doing all this? What force in him kept driving, driving to bring happiness? There was a reservoir of pureness in Joe Campbell. But more than that, he knew how—by design—to kindle team spirit and friendship, how to bring people together. He had done it tonight, and this had to be the purpose of the canoe trip.

"I don't know if I'll be back in time."

"I hope you will," he said sincerely. "We're going down the White River to see the autumn leaves."

Judy wanted to go. He was showing her the way to touch and be touched by her son, giving her ready-made opportunities.

"I'll try," she promised.

As the evening wound down and curfew time approached, Joe stepped to the center of the living room and made a low-key but enthusiastic speech about the game, standing next to each boy as he described that player's part in winning. He circled slowly, missing no one, leaving no vital play unrecounted. One by one, all were honored.

Then he called for "last dance" and chose Leona as his partner—Leona, who had been sitting to one side, enjoying the clamor and the music, tapping her foot and sampling French dip.

Judy stood in the kitchen doorway, pleased. She could not make out what Campbell was saying to Leona, but her mother-in-law responded with vigor and delight.

Later, still stimulated by the foreign sensation of joy, Judy lay wide-eyed in bed, her body pulsing with energy. Things long hidden seemed to dislodge themselves from the alcoves of her brain, flow clearly to her. Feelings of youth. And strength. And hope.

Near two o'clock Kevin crept through the darkness and sat down on the edge of her bed. They held hands tightly, saying nothing.

CHAPTER 10

NEW YORK, NEW YORK

Thursday, September 28, 1972

THE PEOPLE! All leaving the airport building in the same crush, a herd of cattle stampeded through narrow pens. Judy steeled her bones and nervously pressed her purse a little tighter under one arm.

It wasn't supposed to be like this—the sudden exodus, tempers flaring and adrenaline high. But the activists had been outfoxed. United States government and military officials had taken the POWs into custody as soon as their plane landed. The antiwar delegation, which had escorted the men from Hanoi through Moscow and Copenhagen, had unexpectedly seen their charges wrested from them and whisked away to military hospitals.

Judy was swept in a current of bodies, out the glass doors and along the pavement. Dozens—hundreds?—of angry faces met hers, some jeering, most silent. She was surprised to see so many waiting to give her hell, waiting to express their contempt for the unsanctioned peace efforts. People surged and pushed at one another in spite of barricades and police officers.

A middle-aged woman in a blue coat ran up to Judy and shook her. "Traitor!" she screamed, her curly hair wild with static electricity in the cold evening. "How dare you side with the enemy?" She wore gold half glasses, and Judy, stunned, did nothing but look into the woman's dark brown eyes which had black, angry pinholes at their centers.

A policeman grabbed the woman and pulled her from Judy.

Friends up ahead were meeting resistance, being bullied. *I should be with them*, she thought. *I should be at the front.* In the Washington demonstrations Judy had often walked ahead of the others. Opponents, no matter how adamant, seemed disinclined to tangle with a POW wife. She was a sacred cow.

Connie Roberts, who appeared suddenly at Judy's elbow, shouted close to her ear, "Let's get out of here!"

They made their way through a forest of fury, feeling the crowd block their passage and then shift and divide to give them room.

An aircraft began to thunder on a nearby runway. The noise seemed to send a fresh pulse of energy along the knots of people. She could notice their faces tighten. Her scalp tingled. Fighting began a few yards away. She couldn't see fully what was happening, but she could glimpse two men tussling.

As she turned to grab Connie's arm, something snared her ankle, and she fell forward helplessly, watching the concrete rise to meet her. Putting her hands out to break the impact, she rolled to one side without a sound. People tripped over her, their shoes striking her back and shoulders. Instinctively she covered her head with her arms.

Now a deliberate kick caught her sharply in the ribs, knocking her breath out and away from her. Dazed, she lay motionless for a few seconds, then scrambled away from the assailant she knew was pursuing her. If only she could get to her feet! Where was Connie? She rose on one knee, looking fearfully toward her attacker. He was already moving away, through the jumble of legs and arms. A man. In a dirty fatigue jacket. Torn jeans. Sneakers so old they had been repaired with adhesive tape.

Rage took over. She stood and began to run after him.

"Judy!" she heard Connie call. "Judy!"

Pain jolted her with every step.

The man paused to glance behind him, and she memorized his face—what there was of it to see. He was unshaven; oily hair hung across his eyes. The eyes! They held no hatred, no feeling of any kind, as though he had been set against her by the mere winding of a key in his back.

She walked toward him with determination. She had digested all the American venom she was going to eat.

He saw this in her. His expression clouded over with resolve. As she charged toward him, he raised a hand and pointed his finger at her, as if willing her to stay away.

She stopped, fixing her gaze on that hand. Clean and manicured. A soft hand. Perched at the wrist, just under his cuff, gleamed an expensive watch.

"That shit!" Connie wailed. "That asshole!"

"Did you see him?" Judy felt shocked and cold. Afraid.

"Yes!"

"He didn't look like he belonged there, did he? He was—sort of—in costume. Did you see his hands? They were real clean. He had a fancy watch."

"God, yes. He was weird."

Connie was turning the car out of the airport lot and onto the darkened highway. Judy tried to control her shivering, but it leaped wildly through her, punctuated by desolate pauses in which she felt empty, parched. Nothing moved inside her. No passion, no memory of loved things. The world had narrowed to the growing lump in her side and the oozing torn place on her knee where her stocking had been ground into her flesh.

She settled against the door, resting her head on the seatback, trying to reason out where she was now, and why.

The only continuity seemed to be Connie. The image of Connie at seven years old came so strongly to Judy: a sturdy, whimsical girl with a smile shaped like a long rectangle. Her Brownie cap was anchored in her home-permed hair by a number of wide bobby pins. On Judy's first day in the new school, entering midyear, she sifted through the staring faces until she found Connie's. Later, when Judy discovered she hadn't brought money for

morning milk, Connie silently deposited her own un-
opened carton on Judy's desk. Chocolate.

She and Connie in the night, winding and unwinding
adolescent secrets, speaking in low tones until there was
nothing more to tell. *There was a time when there was nothing
more to tell,* when life was so simple that everything could
be said in a single long evening. *Judy, at five, lying in bed
after dark,* counting the people she knew. She got to forty-
one. The world was that small.

"You all right?" Connie whispered.

"Yes."

"How did we get here? Did you ever wonder that?"

"We were born at the wrong time. Didn't you ever have
your chart done? If your moon is on the cusp of Libra and
Scorpio or whatever, your life is screwed up from minute
number one."

"Right."

She could hear the smile in Connie's voice. As teenagers
they had tried to uncover their future by every available
means: astrology; the dream dictionary; handwriting analysis; Ouija board. They had gone to a tearoom downtown,
where a motherly woman in a gypsy outfit peered into
their teacups and predicted love. That was the point of it
all. Finding love. Whom would they meet? And when?

"The war," Judy said. "We just got caught in it."

"Did you ever think of that all those times in those nylon
net formals with those—you know—wrist corsages? Did it
ever occur to you there might be a war?"

"No." The lights of the city had gone past, and the other
lamps fanned out to a sprinkling. What kept her fighting
for Ron? Who was he, really? Not a cardboard figure, a
paper doll. Any recollection of her husband had sound
and substance, was three-dimensional, breathed with its
own life. He had done nothing to deserve his present
torment. Picturing him starving, unbathed, had driven
her year by year through the protests and the rallies. Oh,
the beauty of him. She had been ordered to lie in bed
through the third month of her pregnancy for fear of

miscarrying, and Ron had turned it into a celebration. They would have a baby! Together! When he wasn't at work, he was searching cookbooks for dishes that would tempt her; he was singing in the kitchen, bringing her meals on trays that bloomed with varying colors and themes; he was playing cards with her, reading to her. He came home every lunchtime. She listened for the click of the key in the door. He bathed her each day, right in the bed, gently soaping and rinsing, patting dry. Her life with him had been a series of discoveries, finding him on ever-deepening levels. The sparkle of the wedding ring through her bridal veil had been just a beginning. And now ... the tea leaves and the palm readings and the pennies shoved into arcade machines to produce a card describing her "Ideal Love Mate" had come to this: finding him, marrying him, finding him, finding him ... through their many seasons of pleasure. Losing him. Trying to find him again.

"Judy, I'll never give up," Connie said. "I'm right beside you."

But Judy was tired of it all. They had fought the system for so long. She wasn't sure that she could keep going. She hurt. Everywhere.

"You wouldn't back off, would you, Judy? We're going to win. You know that. The bastards'll never stop us."

She would be getting off the bus in a minute. It was loudly grinding its way along the last block. Judy could see the blue, peeling bus station sign. There were college men and women waiting under it—the weekend dates for Homecoming. She glimpsed Doug's brown crew cut.

"Which one is your pin mate?" Ron asked.

"The tall one with the navy sweater. Which one is Cindy?"

"There. In the pink coat."

"She's pretty."

The bus lurched into a lower gear and rumbled to a halt. Judy and Ron gathered their belongings and stood up, waiting for the aisle to clear.

"Thanks for the good conversation," Ron said. "Four hours on

*a crate like this can kill you if you don't have somebody interesting
to talk to."*

She nodded. "It was nice meeting you."

*Darn! Lucky, lucky Cindy Whoever. I hope you appreciate this
guy Ron.*

*"Maybe I'll see you Sunday," he offered. "Are you taking the bus
back?"*

"Yes. Eleven o'clock."

"Hey—me too."

*Ron slipped into the aisle and let Judy get in front of him. Doug
was waving at her through the window. She dutifully waved back.
Cindy stood to one side, smiling, holding her fur collar up around
her ears. She had yellow hair, like Ron's. Petite. That's what she
was. Judy recognized in herself the seed of jealousy.*

"Well, have fun now," he said as they navigated the steps.

*And then they were in the jabbing wind, walking away from
each other.*

"No. I won't quit. You can count on it."

"Double promise?" Connie asked, using a term from
their childhood.

"Triple promise."

"Good. We're almost home. How're you feeling?"

"Better, I guess."

"What the hell kind of animal would do a thing like that
to you anyway?"

HEMPSTEAD, NEW YORK

"THE GOVERNMENT, that's who," Grant Roberts said, pacing the living room.

Judy winced as Connie rubbed her back. Judy had
pulled her sweater up to the bra line, and Connie was
spreading Ben-Gay along Judy's ribs.

"Oh, now, Grant . . ." Judy began. The government?

Could it be? Hardly. The government wouldn't set upon its own people, would it? A memory flickered: Judy in a peace march to the Pentagon; armed soldiers on every building she passed.

"Why wouldn't they wear disguises?" Grant struck the air with his fist. "They've got a tap on our phone."

"Grant, we don't know that for sure," Connie said pleadingly. "Come and sit down."

He perched on the edge of an armchair, patting his pockets for a cigarette, finding none. He took one from a ceramic box on the coffee table and lit it; inhaled hungrily, blowing the smoke out his nose.

Judy studied Grant's features. He had changed a great deal during his Air Force service in Vietnam. At Connie and Grant's wedding seven years ago, Judy had decided that Grant was movie star material. That square, symmetrical face, the unwavering gaze and dimpled chin. The hair of his head and his mustache had been the embodiment of his vitality, alive with sheen and wave. But now Grant's appearance implied he had been very ill. His eyes were sunken, ringed with shadow. The sensual, virile hair had gone limp and thin.

"I've been there, Judy." He wagged the cigarette at her. "I've been there and back, and I'm here to tell you about it."

"It's over now, Grant. Can't we just . . ." Connie began.

"No!" Grant exploded, jumping from his seat. He went to the bay window and looked out at the neighboring lights of their lane. "Was getting me back the only thing, the only reason you were in this?" he accused Connie.

"Of course not," she said, wiping the ointment off her fingers with Kleenex and putting the cap back on the tube. "But maybe you need some time to . . . not talk about it. To let it fade a little."

"Hell," he said, putting his cigarette out in a nearby ashtray. Judy noted absently that he had taken only a few puffs. "Don't you see? They send me home, and they think it's over. But it's not over for me."

Judy edged her sweater down and leaned back against the sofa pillows. "Tell us then."

Connie opened her mouth. Judy put a hand on her knee. "I want to hear."

"Judy . . ." Grant came over and knelt next to the coffee table, thinking. "Judy," he said, looking tired and defeated, "I've been back three weeks, and I'm still over there. You know?"

Judy nodded.

"You're doing the right thing, Judy. The government isn't straight. We've gotta make everyone know it."

"Excuse me," Connie interrupted, getting up, "but I've heard this before." She went quickly to their bedroom and closed the door.

"She wants me to relax." Grant tapped his temple. "I've been . . . not able to relate to the kids." He glanced toward the end of the house, where they must surely be sleeping by now. "But I can't get my . . . balance. Remember that when Ron comes home. It takes awhile."

Judy swallowed hard.

"The government lied. About the bombing. The dams and dikes. You know? They lied. We were bombing all that shit. All the time. I'd pick up the paper and read official comments about the bombing. That we weren't doing . . . you know."

"Yes."

"We were."

Affirmation and fear stirred in Judy. Grant's testimony had given her another puzzle piece. Bit by bit she was building a picture she had always suspected was there: Immoral war. Mismanaged. Ill-guided. A war that had never been declared by the American Congress or sanctioned by its people. A war directed by shadowy things in government. Not the shiny, well-dressed faces that smiled from the newspaper, but something under all that.

"I should have quit. Other guys did, and took the heat. I didn't have the balls to quit. It was so useless. I was killing their kids, and I couldn't say, 'no, I won't do it anymore.' "

Tears began to spill from his lower lids and run down his cheeks across the stubble of his whiskers.

September 29, 1972

"Do you think something's broken?" Grant asked as they walked through his vegetable garden in the early morning.

Judy reached back and put a hand to her spine, triggering again the throbbing tenderness.

"I don't think so. My blazer saved me. But I sure am sore."

They were stepping lightly between rows of spent tomato plants and brown, brittle bean stalks which curled along a wooden trellis.

"Connie said the garden was great this summer. I'm sorry I wasn't here for most of it." He bent down to lift some large green leaves and revealed a pumpkin. "The last crop. We've got three of them. There are two more over there." He pointed toward the back of the patch.

"I'm sorry I acted like such an ass last night."

"You didn't," Judy answered.

"Connie thinks I did. You get ripped out of a nightmare and wake up in your own bed, but the nightmare's still real."

"I know."

"Funny thing. We'd be sitting on that little island in the Pacific, playing cards and sunning ourselves. Then—boom—we'd take that big baby up and murder." He shook his head. "On the days we didn't bomb we went up anyway, to dump fuel."

Judy turned to stare at Grant. "What?"

"Dump it in the ocean, come back and play cards."

"Dump it? Why?"

"Allotments. Gotta keep the gas coming. You know?"

"Hey!" Connie appeared on the back porch with the two

girls. They were five and six, barely in school. "We're gonna go now. After I drop the kids off, I'm going on to work."

Grant waved at them. Judy went up to say good-bye.

She put her arm around Connie's shoulders and walked with her through the house to the station wagon parked in the circular driveway out front. The children clambered in—coats and lunch boxes, books and boots.

"You take it easy now," Connie said, hugging Judy gingerly. "Hope that spot gets better, fast."

Judy tried to memorize the sleek raven hair, short and brushed into chic wisps. The slow, sincere smile.

"I'll miss you," Judy told her.

"Take care."

Judy lowered her voice. "I hope everything works out okay with Grant."

"I don't know. He's very different," Connie whispered. "Don't believe everything he says, Judy. He's strange now. . . . He exaggerates, gets his facts mixed up." Her smile had faded.

When Judy entered the house, Grant already had her suitcase and coat sitting next to the door.

"Trying to rush me off?" She laughed.

"We need to go in a couple of minutes, so I can get you to the airport on time."

Judy took a last look around for her belongings and paused at the back picture window, gazing out at the garden.

"I wish it were spring," Grant said. "That's the best time. When you're just turning the earth over, thinking about where to plant what, and you've got those seeds and kernels of corn—a whole feast, right in your hand. You push them down, and you cover them up with that black dirt, each one in its secret hiding place. And you're the only one who knows there's something there. I don't like this time of year." His voice was hoarse. "When it's all done, when they're all picked or rotten. I don't like that.

"Connie thinks I'm crazy," he said, moving behind Judy to put both hands on her hips. Startled, she tried to step away, but he encircled her waist and held her against him, breathing into her hair.

She half fell out of his grasp and backed away from him, toward the front door. He came after her.

"Judy, I just want you to hold me, that's all. Just . . ." He beckoned her toward him. "Put your arms around me. Please. I need that, Judy. Can't you give me that?"

She felt ill, too warm. She had to get out of the house.

When she put her hand on the doorknob, his hand closed over it, pulling it, prying her fingers away. This man was sick. To resist him might be to invite violence.

Judy slowly took Grant's hands in hers, trying to give the illusion of strength, of power over him. In answer, he slammed her against the door with his body. The wound under her ribs sent out sparkles of fire.

Neither of them moved.

A vision of Campbell passed in front of Judy. Campbell. Dispelling her son's bitterness with the amazing gift of his touch.

But what if she were wrong?

Judy reached up then and embraced Grant—one arm around his ribs, the other up over his neck. Hugged him the way she would hug Kevin. Pretending he was Kevin.

He clung to her like a child.

Not daring to speak or to shift her weight lest it be misinterpreted, she stood quietly with Grant for three or four minutes, listening to the torn breathing become calmer, more shallow, feeling the pounding of his heart gradually subside into measured thuds and, finally, into tiny shudders.

He released her and lifted her coat and case.

They walked wordlessly out to the car.

Saturday, September 30, 1972

KEVIN STOOD on the curb in front of his home in the predawn chill, waiting for Joe Campbell. He shoved his hands deep into the pockets of his sweat jacket and stamped his feet. It would be cold this morning out on the river. Mentally he checked his supplies, glancing down at the knapsack he had packed. An extra change of clothes. Matches. Canteen of water. Bug spray. Sandwiches.

Far up the avenue, headlights turned the corner and started toward him. Campbell would be easy to fool at this hour. He sure as heck wasn't going to go up to the door and ring the bell. Not at 6:00 A.M.

Kevin hefted his knapsack and swung one of its straps over his shoulder. With any kind of luck, his mother would never find out that the other parents had gone on the trip. She had suspected nothing when he told her Campbell had changed his mind in favor of team members only.

The approaching car pulled slowly to the side and stopped in front of him. Campbell reached across to open the passenger door, and the car's ceiling light came on. Kevin blinked.

"Hey there, sport!"

"Hi, Coach!" Kevin climbed in and slammed the door.

"Gonna be a big day, huh?"

"You bet!" Kevin could hardly wait. The wide river, the peaceful hours. It would be good.

Campbell leaned forward, looking toward the house. "Where's your mom?"

"Well . . ." Kevin paused. This was no time to hedge. He had to be very offhand about it. "She can't come."

"She can't? Why not?"

"She hurt her back in New York, and she didn't think all that rowing would be good for it."

Campbell touched the dashboard, flicking the light on again and studying Kevin. "You and I could row for her. All she'd have to do is sit in the middle."

Kevin tried to return Campbell's stare. "She's still sleeping. She doesn't want to go. I don't think it would be nice to wake her up."

Campbell turned the light off and got out of the car. "We'll see about that."

Kevin slid down in his seat, resting the back of his head. Jeez! What now? He could only pray that something would intervene. Apprehension made him start to perspire. He felt cold. Campbell had evidently been ringing the bell, for Leona appeared. Kevin could only half see her. He listened. Campbell's voice was low, apologetic.

"Let me go and ask," Kevin heard his grandmother say.

Campbell sat on the stoop to wait, crossing his arms over his knees and resting his head on them. A new wave of uneasiness spread through Kevin. In a minute Leona was back, and Campbell jumped to his feet. Their heads leaned close together as they conferred. Leona was shaking hers. That was a no. Had she awakened his mother or merely answered for her?

Kevin glanced up at his mother's bedroom window. All dark. But if Leona had spoken to her? Then she would know by now. She would realize that he hadn't wanted her to go on this trip, had tricked her and excluded her.

Would serve her right . . . going off to New York with those people that the newspaper said didn't respect our government. Acting like that! He squeezed his eyelids together, looked again toward the front door.

Campbell wasn't there. Neither was Leona. She must have let him in.

"Judy, Major Campbell wants to talk to you for a minute." Leona spoke from the shadows.

Judy stirred in her bed, overcome with sadness. Kevin hadn't been telling her the truth. He didn't want her to go on the team trip.

"Judy." Leona came a little farther into the room. "Could you come down?"

"No. Tell him I'll call him tonight or tomorrow."

"He wants you to go along on the canoe safari."

"I can't."

"But he says all the parents are going."

Judy sat up in bed, squinting at her mother-in-law in the dimness. "Kevin doesn't want me to go, Leona. He told me the other parents weren't invited."

"Oh." She could hear Leona's disappointment—Leona, who wanted everything to be so perfect.

Judy heard the banister creak as Leona went down into the foyer. She got up and pulled her robe around her, walked to the window, waiting to see Campbell return to the car.

A heavy tread shook the stairs, taking them two by two. She whirled to see Campbell's frame fill the doorway.

"Mrs. Greer . . . Judy . . . excuse me. I'm sorry to come up here this way."

"What is it?"

"Could I come in? I want to say something to you. Quietly. Could I come over where you are?"

"All right."

He began to walk slowly toward her. It was so strange. Him. In this room that she'd kept as a museum, a monument to Ron. Life and vitality. Here.

"I'll say it to you straight. I know that Kevin must have lied to you, told you the families weren't going. But they are. And I want you to come."

"He doesn't want me."

"He *does*. He needs you very much. But he's confused."

Campbell's features were becoming more distinct as sun glow began to fill the panes of glass. She saw tenderness and concern.

"Trust me. I'll make it work. Let me help."

"Why should you?" She regarded him carefully, judging the set of his mouth, the honesty of his eyes.

"I know what it feels like to come home to a broken family. I don't want that to happen."

Damn it! Kevin could feel her gaze burning his neck. He sat stiffly in the front of the canoe, staring straight ahead, paddling vigorously. Behind him, at the very back, Joe Campbell used his paddle to guide the vessel. His surprising strength directed it easily. There were places where the current was rapid and battered the lightweight craft and there were other spots close to the shore where trees seemed to grow starkly from the river bottom. Campbell took them all without comment.

Now Kevin could feel the coach stick his paddle vertically into the river and hold it there, trying to slow the swift descent of the boat downstream. Ahead, ten other canoes were spread out along the water: his teammates and their mothers and fathers.

His mother sat quietly in the middle, unable to help in any way because of the big dark yellow bruise at her waist. Why did she have to go those places and do those things? People were bound to hurt her. She continually let herself in for it. Everyone knew who she was. She had even been on television.

Why was she here? He couldn't understand why she had pulled on her jeans and sweat shirt and run out to the car when she knew how he felt!

The kids would tease him when they got the chance, give her the cold treatment all day. It was in the newspaper that she had been part of that thing in New York where the antiwar people had brought some POWs home. She was a criminal. That's the way people thought of it.

"Do you think that's paranoid?" his mom asked now. She must be talking to Campbell. She and Kevin hadn't said a word to each other since they'd left the house.

Campbell took his time in answering. "No. It's entirely possible that the government would like to give you a whack. You're a very recognizable person, not just because you're into the peace efforts, but because you're the wife of a prisoner. They could want to shut you up somehow. Or intimidate you."

"Bullshit," Kevin said. He felt his mother stir, rocking the canoe slightly.

"Another country heard from," Campbell answered with his usual humor. "Tell us, sir. What is your candid opinion?"

"It's a bunch of garbage." Here was his opportunity to let her have it. She wouldn't, she couldn't react much out here with a stranger.

"What makes you say that?" Campbell asked.

Kevin hunched his shoulders and didn't answer.

"Why do you say that, son?" Campbell demanded.

"I think lots of people would want to hurt her. I don't know why you can't just mind your own business."

"Me?" Campbell said.

"No, her."

"Kevin," she said softly. "It is my business."

Kevin could feel himself winding into the old anger. "Why? It makes me ashamed of you."

"It does?" She sounded hurt.

"Yeah. It's a pain in the butt." Now he'd said it, the way he'd wanted to say it for so long.

"Kevin, we'd better talk about this at home," his mother cautioned. Her tone took on the squeaky edge he knew came just before tears.

Kevin and Campbell steered the boat around a giant black log rising ominously from the glittering water.

"Judy, the kid needs to unload all that. Let him dump it out."

"That's all," Kevin growled.

"Go ahead," his mother said, sounding calmer. "Let me have it." Kevin sensed that she was somehow shored up by Campbell's presence.

"All my friends know you're doing those things. It isn't right."

"Your friends care about what I'm doing?"

"It's like you're outside the law. Or like you think you are. Everybody else is doing all this stuff for America, and you're . . . going the other way."

"But I can't just stop, don't you see? It's what I believe."

"Why does it have to be you? You've been doing it for so long. You're giving up everything to it. You're giving up *me*."

She had no answer. They drifted in silence down a placid stretch of river, past hills full of broadleaf trees, thousands of little paintbrushes dipped in gold and red; past homes perched on knolls and tucked into hollows. They glided smoothly under stone bridges. When they glimpsed the white massive elegance of the new Indianapolis museum, his mother said, "I was an art history major. I always wanted to work in an art museum like that one."

"Why don't you?" Joe Campbell suggested. And the subject—as Kevin knew it would be—had been changed.

At noon they all slid their canoes up onto the bank and climbed a short way into a flat glade. Judy stood shyly to one side while Kevin plunged into a gathering of boys, sharing his sandwiches and chattering excitedly. There was meaning to the way he put his back to her. The other parents were congenial, but clustered in a way that made Judy know they were friends, had met each other before this. She opened a plastic bag and took out her sandwich, sat down with her back against a tall pin oak. Campbell came and sat beside her.

"It'll be okay," he said, staring happily up through the tent of color.

"I'm sorry I'm here."

Campbell drank milk directly from a small thermos. "He has to say it to you, you know. He has to get it out. That's how it'll heal up. Tell him how you feel, too."

Judy felt her cheeks begin to flame. She put the remainder of the sandwich back in the plastic bag and closed it.

"What else happened in New York?"

"What else?"

"Other than the airport trouble. There's something you haven't told me."

How could he know that? Amazed, she tried to read his green eyes.

"Not simple, is it?"

"You're not simple." She laughed. "Definitely. How do you know all these things?"

"I know you, Judy." There was intimacy in the way he spoke. "What, then?"

"A man. A friend," she said, idly playing with acorns and twigs. "He just came back from the war. This is going to sound stupid."

She got up. Campbell rose, too, waiting.

Judy shook her head. "I don't know how to tell it."

"Straight out." He crumpled the aluminum foil from his lunch and shoved it into his pants pocket.

They strolled a few feet into the thickening woods.

"He's married to an old classmate of mine. He's been through a lot, in Vietnam. They argue. The morning I left, she wasn't there. At their house. He asked me to put my arms around him." She stopped walking, glanced up at Campbell, gauging his reaction. "I did it."

He shrugged. "This upsets you?"

"It sounds silly."

"Not silly. But not something to be upset over."

"I wasn't the one who should have been doing the comforting, you see? I feel sad for them."

He nodded, and she knew they both were thinking of the same thing: Kevin and him on the football field.

"The wrong people are holding all the wrong people, aren't they?" Joe smiled.

She closed her eyes.

"It's not bad, you know. At a certain point we can become lost—irretrievably lost—unless, at the last minute, we reach out. Sometimes it isn't the right person who happens to be there, who *can* be there." His voice had gradually dropped to a whisper. "But it's the person who can save us. So we have to go ahead. That's not the time to be afraid and do nothing."

She wanted him to touch her then. But the air was filled with the laughter of young people and the pleasant calling out of adults as they cleaned up the picnic area and prepared to board the canoes.

CHAPTER 12

"OVER HERE, Kevin!" Campbell motioned to the seat at the back of the canoe. "We're going to mix it up a little this time. Justin, why don't you get in here with Kevin?" He put Justin at the front and helped Judy into the middle while the boys leaned side to side for balance.

"We're going to mix it up, everybody!" Campbell declared, trotting along the bank, assigning people to canoes.

Kevin sat stiffly, waiting for the signal to shove off. Why had the coach put him and his mother in with Justin Helms? Rats. Justin had been the roughest to Kevin on the field and had ignored him the rest of the time.

The crowd paired off, climbing into the canoes. Campbell got into one with Mrs. Helms. Mr. Helms rode with Andy Warner. It was all goofed up. Justin would hate this. Kevin hated it, too.

As they pulled away from the coolness of the bank, out onto the river, Kevin gave serious thought to swamping the canoe. He trailed a hand in the icy ripples. Bad weather to overturn and have to swim to shore.

"Okay! Line up," Campbell shouted. "We're going to race to the next landing. You'll see some wooden steps. On the right."

Eleven canoes (Kevin counted them) maneuvered into position across the brilliant water.

"You characters in place?" Campbell's words skipped and echoed like skimming stones.

Kevin assessed the faces around him. They all seemed pleased, excited. He couldn't see Justin's reaction.

"Get ready. Get set. And . . . go!"

All the paddles dipped into the water at once—a series of splashes piercing the air. Kevin pushed his paddle into the deep and the canoe sprang forward. Justin worked the other side. The guy was fast! Kevin felt a burst of exhilaration.

Andy Warner's craft was taking the lead. Kevin leaned into his strokes. He noticed Justin looking back to check cadence. Although they were sprinting along, the canoe had a dangerous rock. They weren't synchronized.

"Should I set the rhythm?" his mother asked.

Embarrassment shot through Kevin. *She should be quiet.*

"Great," Justin replied.

She began with measured beat to call out, "Now . . . now . . . now . . ."

Other canoes were ahead of them. In one, Sam Owens and his dad started to turn their boat in a slow circle. Easy to do. They couldn't coordinate their strokes. Their laughter floated to Kevin. Beside them, a couple of teams paused to spray water at each other by slapping paddles on the choppy surface.

Kevin's canoe and two more moved significantly ahead. One was Campbell's. Was Justin enjoying this?

"Now . . . now . . . now . . . now . . ." His mother kept the pace.

"We'll show you who's boss," Campbell hollered, grinning, his face red from the strain.

The heck you will, Kevin thought. If Campbell's face was already flushed, Kevin had an inkling that he and Justin could beat the coach.

"Put your paddle where your mouth is," Kevin shouted back. Campbell opened his mouth comically wide.

Justin's mother, a thin blond lady with long hair wrapped around her head, whooped with delight and dug into the water with renewed vigor, helping Campbell for all she was worth.

The two canoes were way out in front now. Kevin's arm began to sting with the effort. He could feel a gruesome pinch, a gnawing sometimes when he worked hard or when the weather changed suddenly. The bullet had missed the bone, they said, but a phantom bullet ate at his marrow.

He gripped the paddle tighter. It was a day for winning.

"You are getting very sleepy," Campbell yelled. "The paddles are getting very heavy. You must put them dowwwn."

They were number one. Campbell and Mrs. Helms had fallen about three yards behind.

"How far is this place?" Justin asked.

"I don't know," Kevin said, watching for the steps.

"Now . . " his mother called. "Now . . . now . . . now . . ."

Campbell's canoe dogged them, a sticky shadow. They moved along for several minutes in crystal silence except for the cadence. Wind filled the arms of Kevin's jacket. His shirtfront billowed and fluttered. He was flying. The canoe was flying.

The steps came into sight, cockeyed and dilapidated, climbing down a hillside through a stand of elms. Not far to go. As if in answer to this final challenge, Campbell's craft began to gain steadily on theirs.

"You're surrounded," Campbell growled. "Come out with your hands up."

It wasn't that far. They could make it. Kevin knew they could.

His mother spoke more loudly, urgently. "Now . . . now . . ."

The two canoes approached the stairs. Justin and Kevin slammed their paddles into the water over and over. They were one being, the three of them. Kevin could feel vibrant communication darting along their shoulders. In the corner of his eye he saw the other canoe slipping back.

With a final surge of determination they reached the steps, smacking into the lowest one so hard the canoe bounced away and crashed up and down. Slosh-whoosh-slosh-slosh. A second later Campbell's canoe barreled into the side of the weathered steps, banging and tilting their already shuddering craft. For a second their surprised faces regarded each other with fear. Would they all tip over?

The canoes settled to a gentle hopping.

Justin let out a victorious cry, and Kevin heard himself scream in triumph. His mother gave a totally undignified and freeing shriek, reaching up to pound Justin affectionately on the back.

He didn't have to see Justin's eyes to know that something astonishing had happened: an overture of friendship, strung delicately, spun like a soft web across the afternoon.

The rest of the canoes came gliding in. Good people, smiling. More strands. Light threads. Intertwined. Swinging, glistening in the sun.

"Do you remember anything about when Dad was captured?"

"What do you want to know that for?" Kevin stood in the tree shadows, his arms laden with dry branch pieces and green sticks long enough to toast marshmallows.

His mother came closer and walked by his side as they looked for a few more scraps. All about them were the sounds of people searching for firewood in the evening forest. In the distance Andy Warner tuned up his guitar.

"I want us to talk, Kevin."

No way, he thought. It couldn't lead to anything good. It never had. "I don't want to."

"Why?"

"Let's go back. We have enough wood."

"Please talk to me." She ran to get in front of him, stood waiting.

"Mom, I don't have anything to say." Was this going to set her off?

"Do you remember when Dad was put in prison? Tell me if you remember."

"I remember."

"You've never mentioned it."

"Come on." He jogged around her and headed for the camp.

She grabbed him by the arm, pulled him to a stop.

"You'll cry, Mom. I don't want to hear it."

"I won't. Why do you think I will?"

"You always do."

He was on his knees, leaning over the side of the bathtub, his hands deep in the warm water. As he swished them back and forth, the water toys bobbed and clacked against one another: a long white steamboat with red trim, a pink plastic yacht, a submarine with a bubble top, a frog and a seal that flapped their legs when Kevin wound them up.

The doorbell rang. He listened for his mother's cheery voice, the rumbling tones of some salesman or the excited pitch of a neighbor lady.

The bell rang again: two round notes, an O and an O. Kevin got up quickly, dripping water from his hands across his shoes and socks.

He went into the hall and peered down the steps. There was a little window in the front door; his mother had covered it with a lacy curtain, but he could see the heads of two people—tall. Men?

The emptiness of the house flooded to him. He could always tell when she was here and when she wasn't. He hurried into the bathroom again and looked out the window. His mother was pulling clothes off the line, plucking the pins up one by one until she had a fistful, throwing the pins into a paper bag, stuffing sheets and towels and underwear into a square bin.

He unlocked the window and slid it up. "Mom! There's somebody at the door!"

"Okay," she called over her shoulder, taking the last few washcloths. As she walked away, the rope continued to jump and ripple. The clothespin bag rattled lightly as she picked it up and carried it in with her.

Who was it? Kevin came halfway down the steps to see. His mother smiled at him as she whished past, untying her apron and laying it on a table.

She opened the door. A soundless explosion hit her. She took three or four steps backward and covered her ears against . . . What did she hear? He didn't hear anything. There were two men standing on the porch. They were both in uniform like his father. Army. Green. That was Army.

She gripped both doorknobs, the one on the inside and the one on the outside, sank to her knees, her head bowed. Were these bad men? Did she think they were going to hurt her?

Kevin's neck began to pulse in alarm. He scrambled down the steps, but before he could reach his mother, one of the men put his hands under her arms and lifted her slowly.

"It's all right," he said to her. "Judy . . . he's probably alive. We'll bring him back."

The other man seemed to know his mother, too; he called her by her first name and helped her into the living room.

The door was still open. Kevin, knowing that more bad things would come in, closed it quickly and put the gold chain on it.

But a terrible sadness was already in there. With them. The only safe place was by his mother. He ran to her, past the enemies in the green uniforms, tried to make her move over so that he could sit in the same chair. She didn't look at him. She was staring at the intruders.

Kevin patted her cheek and chin, trying to get her attention, but she did not respond. There was a vast, frightening silence in her. The skin of her arm was cool, a stranger's arm next to his.

It was something about his father. He knew.

He got up and went to the front door, undid the chain and stood desperately searching the porch steps and the flower-bordered walkway. He had the scary feeling that his father had been out there but was now far down the empty street. Moving away from him. Not looking back. Being drawn toward the colorless sky.

Kevin suddenly focused on her face. She was reading him with horror.

"Is it so bad, what you remember?" Her eyes narrowed in anguish.

"You left me," Kevin said. "He left me. And then you left me." He started for the campsite.

"Kevin . . ." She stayed at his side. "I didn't mean to . . . I never meant to leave you. I didn't really leave you. I'm still here."

The ground ahead of him was blurry and uncertain. He slowed down, glanced at her.

Her lips were trembling. Soon would come the wall of grief. "What can I do?" she pleaded. "Tell me one thing I can do."

"Don't cry when I'm crying. It makes me feel like a jerk. Like I shouldn't be asking you for anything."

"All right," she said. "I can do that."

It was almost over, the hot dogs and the marshmallows, the jokes and ghost stories. In another few minutes the kids would be cleaning up, putting earth on the fire.

Through the shimmering flames, Kevin studied the figures across from him. Andy, still plucking his guitar. He knew one basic chord and about four melodies, but that had been enough for a lot of noisy singing. Mr. Helms. What would it be like to go home with your father? To go home with your mother and your father and close the door? Campbell, telling an alligator yarn, flapping his hands together like jaws and looking around for a victim.

And his mother. Tonight her face was joyful. She had told stories and hummed to the guitar. He had been impressed with her. Surprised. He was glad she had come with them after all. The lie he had told her prickled like a burr.

Kevin would take all of the day's images home with him, open them in the privacy of his room, let the memories pop out and dance.

"Okay, you guys, we've got to start clearing up," Campbell said.

Andy hit one final sour chord, smacking the strings and pulling the guitar strap off over his head. "Wait," he urged. "There's something else." He looked at Sam, who reached into his pack for a tin box. Candy?

Sam gave Kevin a half smile. He pried up the lid with his fingertips, removed a skinny, glinting object and passed the box to Mr. Helms. Mr. Helms passed it to Justin, who also took . . .

Bracelets. Kevin could see now. He knew exactly what it was the boys were selecting. He knew the shape. This bracelet would have the name of Ronald Greer on it. And the date of his capture.

The fire seemed hotter than ever. Kevin's cheeks boiled. His back was freezing.

The box went on, around the circle, each boy selecting a bracelet. How? Why? Kevin's gaze shifted to Campbell, who was looking down at his hands. He was the source.

The container had made its round and was approaching Kevin. He accepted it, feeling intense pressure at the back of his throat. The boys watched him carefully, apprehensively. He did not sense in them anything false.

Kevin stared into the box. There was one bracelet left. He and his mother and Leona all had these bracelets, but he had never worn his. It had slid to the back of a dresser drawer under old baseball cards and school papers. He had been afraid, had forsaken his father in this way because he couldn't take the heat—the reaction of the kids.

Now he drew out the last bracelet and put it on.

It felt good.

CHAPTER 13

Sunday, October 1, 1972

HER KNEE WAS loosening up, and the rib pain had eased to a twinge. Judy started out slowly, jogging along the sidewalk. About her, in the new day, leaves were lifted from the ground by sudden powerful winds, thrown toward the sky like confetti. She began to cut across open lots, heading for the fields beyond.

Instinctively she turned and took a last look at her house. A station wagon was parked in front of it. Red. Campbell's! What would he be doing here? She started back, alternately walking and running. He was on the porch now, carrying a large paper bag; he set it down, rang the bell.

She crossed the street and called to him. When he faced her, smiling, she felt again the pull of his magnetism.

"Hi, Judy."

"Good morning!"

"Kevin left some stuff in my car. On the trip. I brought it along. Thought he might be looking for it." Campbell put his hands on the porch railing, swung himself over it with ease and dropped the five feet onto the grass.

Judy laughed. "I'm impressed."

"I was hoping to impress you. Where are you going?"

"My daily constitutional."

"Can I go along?"

"Well . . . sure."

"Where are the troops?" He gestured toward the house.

"Leona takes Kevin to Sunday school and church."

"And your church is the great outdoors."

"You got it."

"Hey, I've been thinking about the art museum and what you said. Remember?" he asked as they trotted toward the fields. "Why don't you go to work there?"

"You going to arrange it?"

They smiled at each other.

"You arrange it, Judy. I bet they'd take you in a minute. It might be your calling."

She thought of the art palace, its polished chambers, high glass cases. Mexican pottery with eyeless birds and expressionless gods. Medieval tapestries crowded with serious citizens. Chinese rose petal jars. The pale Renaissance madonnas, blue-hooded and backed by solid halos. Maybe she would.

"What's *your* calling, Coach?"

"What do you mean?"

"Your job—at the post."

"Oh. Right now I'm a troubleshooter."

"At the Finance Center?"

"Mainly. Limited assignment. Just working some things out. How far are we going?" he panted.

"As a defender of our nation you're supposed to be in great shape," she teased.

"This defender of our nation paddled eleven miles in a canoe yesterday. Where's the finish line?"

She pointed at a lone tree halfway down the meadow. "I go around that. Then I start back."

"Any cow pies out here?"

She began to giggle. "Just the one on your shoe."

He looked down in disgust, but his shoes were clean.

"Uh!" He grinned and wiggled a finger at her. "You got me on that one."

They were rounding the tree now. A slowly forming vision of Joe Campbell disturbed her. They were in her bed, making love. The delicious morning settled over and around them.

"Thinking what?" Campbell said.

She couldn't look at him. He would know. "About the good things you've done for us. I do thank you, Joe."

"Judy, listen. I'm not doing anything for you that you couldn't do for yourself."

"You've made Kevin happier."

"Maybe so. But what I mean is, there's no secret to it. All that fun is just there—waiting to be picked. Like apples on a tree. What difference does it make whether I pick 'em and hand them to you or whether you pick them yourself? Just as long as they get picked. You see?"

Could that be right? Could she have done these things without Campbell? No. Intervention. That's what had occurred.

And how could a man like this have lost his family? Why? They ran in silence down widening lanes, startling the birds and squirrels.

"Tell me about your wife," she said, turning to look at him.

His eyes reflected old grief. "She didn't wait."

"You were away?"

"Unaccompanied tour. I got off the plane. Expected to see her. A man, a military representative, took me aside and told me she had filed for divorce. That's the first I knew of it."

Guilt trembled in Judy. This is what she had intended for Ron. This is how it turns out.

"And your children?" She was guessing.

"Went with her. She was miserable, see? Couldn't handle the loneliness. I was gone for more than a year. She found somebody else. He was only too glad to help. To break up the marriage."

They were back on the pavement, jumping the cracks in the sidewalk like children, sprinting along past Sunday papers and quiet, curtained windows, empty driveways.

"I wouldn't want that to happen to anyone," he said pointedly.

They were approaching the house. Should she ask him in? Would it be interpreted as an invitation to an affair? Did she want that?

She had perhaps thirty seconds to decide.

Hadn't she been deciding it for five years, toying with the notion, pushing it around and around? She had stood alone against it all. And now . . . this man: Joe Campbell. Loving and good to her son; direct and kind with her. In their deepest well of isolation, she and Kevin had been unexpectedly lifted. Nurtured, with no price exacted in return.

Judy paused beside Joe, who was fishing in his pocket for car keys. "Would you like . . . will you have . . . some coffee?"

Judy's fingers felt stiff. She dropped things. Coffee grounds fell all over the counter; water was spilled on the stove.

Joe came and stood behind her. Close. They did not speak. He put his hands on the counter, one on each side of her. She could feel the heat of him. When she turned to him, her heart seemed to shift, throwing her off-balance. No mistaking his intent. He studied her with powerful affection and with passion.

He caught the back of her hair and held onto it, as though he were afraid she would twist away from him. His lips met hers lightly. Stunned by the reality of his touch, his warm, fragrant breath, Judy drew back a little. He slid his arm all the way around her neck, cradling her head in his elbow so that she could not retreat. *Oh, God. Is this really happening? What will I do?* She closed her eyes.

He laid his cheek against hers, encircled her waist with his other arm. Her body started to respond. Pleasure tingled across her breasts. It was all right. No one could see them through the window. The nearest house was out of sight through a tangle of leaves.

She took him to her, accepting the strength of him. He kissed her mouth. An urgent, adoring kiss. She ran her tongue along his lips, investigating the corners of his mouth, delighting in the scent of his skin.

He kissed her again, this time quivering slightly. His hand found the small of her back and pressed her belly to his. She could feel through their clothing the slow, telling rise of him. There was an answering flood of weakness in her. She wanted him. No matter what.

And there was time.

"Judy," he whispered. "Come upstairs."

He led her into the hall. On the third or fourth step, she sat down, dazed. He knelt in front of her, caressing her breasts, kissing her eyelids. He helped her to her feet and half carried her to the bedroom. Her bed was unmade, the rumpled sheets thrown over the end of it, the blanket heaped on the floor. There was no sound but the sigh of fabric as he shed his shirt and carefully tugged her blouse off over her head. These mechanical things were slowing her down, making her fearful. She realized she was listening for the slam of a car door. If Leona and Kevin . . .

They sat on the edge of the bed, bare-chested and suddenly self-conscious. The room seemed cool.

"Joe, I can't . . ." she began, but he put a finger to her mouth.

And then she remembered: He was golden. He wore an aura. Nothing bad could happen while she was with him. He had seen her through this far. His magic would not leave her.

They undressed themselves and lay close to each other in a shaft of sunlight. What would he expect? Who should she be? Her only experience was with Ron, a straightforward and generous lover.

And about birth control?

He pressed his lips between her breasts and began to lick her nipples gently. The honesty of Joe Campbell came to her in his lovemaking; his caring enveloped her. Still, it was all unfamiliar and disorienting. The shape of his body, the weight of him.

"What about the . . . Do you have . . ."

"Yes. Don't worry." She could hardly hear his words.

He took her with surprising force. All the wires that had tethered her to the reference points of her life snapped free. Shaken, she responded with her whole being, wrapping her legs around his back, reaching for all of him, wanting to possess him totally. Wanting him to possess her in a way that would blot out everything else.

She buried her face in his neck, hungrily bit at his shoulder and sucked on it, savoring his salty sweetness. They rocked slowly back and forth, pausing to study each other's eyes. Twice she thought he was going to speak to her, but he did not. She ran her hands down his muscled back, stretching her legs against and around his, taking him, taking him. She wanted to tell him. To tell him something. Her feelings for him. But what could she say? They were in it only for the pleasure. That was understood. Strange, to have such intimacy and not to use the love words.

He was moving with more determination, and she could feel herself bearing down on the exquisite warmth of him.

He was waiting. Waiting for her.

He was not Ron. The enormity of what she was doing came to her like a slap. She struggled under him. He sensed her withdrawal, looked—bewildered—into her face.

"Judy," he said in a husky voice. "Let go. Judy. Oh, won't you ever . . ."

He shoved his arm suddenly under her buttocks and lifted her to him. A moan escaped her, and then a deeper one. She stiffened, clutching at him, losing herself to the dark, shuddering force that overtook her. She would kill for this. Nothing would stop this. It was hers. Hers. This man was. Hers.

The wave of feeling began to subside. But he was still straining inside her.

Ron. Leona. Kevin. The fabric of Judy's life closed itself quietly around her, made her start in Joe's arms, against his insistent pushing. *If she got up now, it could be said not to have happened at all.* She tried to roll to one side, under him, but it was too late. He drew his breath audibly, thrust his other arm under her shoulders and crushed her to him, striking her. Striking her, it seemed like. Striking her.

She twisted with him, answering his wordless cry with her own. She was at the center, the very center of his life. For this moment he needed her beyond all reason. She was his. There was no going back.

CHAPTER 14

Tuesday, October 3, 1972

"DUTY, HONOR, country," his grandmother began. Kevin shifted uneasily. The prevailing color in the cemetery was gray and reminded him of ashes. Even her hair was gray, and her skin, perhaps because she did not use makeup, had a grayish cast. He wished his mother would hurry up and get there.

Leona was not a scary person, did not usually make him feel like backing away. But on this occasion she stood solemn eyed with a black-ribboned wreath hung over her forearm and clutching her Bible.

"As you know, today is your granddaddy's birthday, and I always remember him like this. Wherever I am, I go to the nearest military graveyard to lay some flowers and think about him."

Yes, she had done this two years ago when she stayed with them. And the two years before that. Kevin thought it was probably the third time he had been to Fort Harrison's graveyard with her. Maybe even the fourth. One of those times, he was sure, his father had been here with them.

"It's important that you listen to me," she said, putting her back to the sprinkling of sun which fell through the trees. She examined his face the way she used to check to see if he'd washed it. "Do you know what I mean when I say 'duty, honor, country'? That's the Army motto. You know that."

"Umhum."

"And every word in it really means something—especially to us, because our history is in this great Army. And because of what we're doing right now . . . waiting for your dad. We don't want him to be disappointed in how we have acted."

Maybe there was some way he could tune her out, turn

the volume down and just kind of float through her lecture.

"Look at me."

He met her blue eyes. They were in contrast to the demanding words. Soft. She had always been soft on him.

"Honor is the one I want to talk to you about. That's the one where you're having trouble."

He squared his shoulders in defense.

Leona put a hand on his hair and spoke directly to him. "Honor has everything to do with who we are. We must always conduct ourselves honorably. What I'm saying is, I know you're getting into the habit of not telling the truth."

Kevin felt warm pangs creep along his jawbone.

"We can't have that, Kevin. That has to stop. Now, I know all the newfangled psychology says that a person has reasons, and I'm sure you feel you have your reasons. But that's not good enough. That's too simple. It's too easy to wiggle out of the responsibility that way. We all have reasons right now—for feeling unhappy—but ... I'll bring it right down to basics." She squeezed his scalp so that he couldn't look anywhere but at her. "You're a bright boy, and you *can* control what you're doing. And I want you to *stop lying*. Do you understand me?"

He tried to nod, but her hand was heavy, pushing down on him. His neck felt as if it were getting fatter and redder.

"Do you?"

"Yes."

"Your country and your government and your army are based on honor. Lies are not told. Ever. They are not acceptable."

She let up slightly on the pressure, and he was able to glance past her at the scattered tombstones, weather-smooth and tilted but neatly kept. His eyes followed the line of pointy tops along the cemetery's wrought-iron fence. A small spot, this burial ground. Tight. That was it, always. Every place had a wall or a fence. And most of the time all he wanted was to *get out*.

Behind him, the whir of his mother's car engine grew

louder as she slowed close to them and parked in the street. Leona released his head, and all his blood seemed to rush to it as though she had been blocking his circulation with a clamp, a steel hat.

"Remember," she whispered as they heard the gate open.

"Hallo!" his mother called. She came and stood with them, unsmiling. Was she there strictly to please Leona? Kevin suspected so. She shoved her hands into the pockets of her coat and looked at the grass as Leona took an index card out of the Bible and began to read in halting phrases, tinged with emotion.

"They that love beyond the world, cannot be separated by it. Death cannot kill what never dies. Nor can spirits ever be divided that love and live in the same Divine Principle; the Root and Record of their Friendship. If absence be not death, neither is theirs. Death is but crossing the world, as Friends do the Seas; they live in one another still."

Wind cut a path between the stones. His mother pushed back a blowing strand of hair and tucked it behind an ear. Leona slid the wreath from her arm and laid it ceremonially upon a flat, square marker. Whose grave was that? He hadn't noticed the inscription, and now it was hidden. Was that all? Just that brief passage? A funny thing for her to choose. Friendship. That's what it had been about. Were married people friends?

His mother's features blazed in contrast with the lifeless colors around her. Her cheeks were pink-pink; her lips, a deep red. She looked good. Better than she had for a long time. And now he felt able to understand her just a little because of what his grandmother had read and the way his mother had bowed her head when she was listening to it. She was his father's best friend. Mother and father. They are best friends together. Why hadn't he thought of it before? That's why she let herself be kicked. Not for love only.

He sensed that the friendship part must be unbelievably strong. Like thick, wet ropes. Like tigers.

CHAPTER 15

Wednesday, October 11, 1972

HE APPEARED so suddenly that it shocked her. She stepped back, bumping against the library shelves, clutching her books to her stomach.

"Why have you been avoiding me?" Campbell had her cornered. She stood in his shadow.

He pressed so close to her that all the reasons she had amassed for not seeing him again seemed feeble. If only he'd back up, she might be able to think of them.

"What's the matter?"

Judy scanned the aisles. Empty. "I'm . . . well . . . embarrassed." It was a whisper.

He shook his head. "I don't want you to feel that way."

"I do."

Sadness gathered in his eyes. "I'm sorry."

"My mistake."

"You think of it as a mistake?"

"Yes."

"Don't do that to yourself."

She edged away, but he moved right with her.

"Are you afraid I'm going to take my pound of flesh, make you pay somehow?"

"Keep your voice down." She glanced around the deserted reading room.

His gaze rested on her hair and flickered lightly over her face. The dense, lingering scent of their lovemaking returned to her. Honeysuckle and lilac. Pushcarts of fruit mellowing in city summer sun.

Two women, obviously a mother and daughter, came through the doorway and began searching the stacks. Joe motioned Judy toward the front desk. They checked out their books, emerged from the heat and glare into a gusty night. She buttoned her coat.

"Are you parked around back?" he asked.

"Yes."

"Let's put our books in the car and walk for a while."

She hesitated.

"Please." He took the books from her and strode away under the faint sparkle of the streetlamps. She could see his outline and the outline of the wagon, could hear the door open and solidly shut. Then he was back, taking her by the arm, steering her across the street into pools of blackness along the post green. She could hardly see where they were going, but she could feel the spongy, moisture-clogged leaves springing under her shoes.

"Why didn't you speak to me at the game Friday night? I wanted to share it with you. Wasn't it a great one? Kevin had some fantastic footwork. He's so special. A corker. This team's gonna win it, Judy. The whole thing. I just know it. They're really pulling together now. They can take this city. You watch and see." He slid his hand along her neck, under her hair.

Judy . . . Let go. Oh, won't you ever . . .

"Why did you look the other way? Why wouldn't you talk to me?"

"People will see. Leona."

"How could she know? She'll never know it from me."

"She'd see it in my expression. She's sharp."

He paused, leaned his forehead gently against hers. She thought she could hear her heart beating. Did he hear it?

"How long are you going to bite the bullet, Judy?"

"As long as it takes." She might as well finish it. "I'm not being fair to you, Joe. I don't want to hurt you. But . . . I don't love you."

"Judy . . ." His tone was kind. "Listen. I don't love you either. But I do care about you. It happened. All right? Can't you let it be what it is? Neither of us is trying to fool the other. I'll never ask you for anything. Now or later."

"And when Ron comes home?"

"You know how I feel about that."

"But will you feel that way then?"

"Will you?"

"I will."

He laughed. "Is this a Mexican standoff?"

"I love Ron."

"Okay. But love yourself, too. I'll bet you didn't even go over to the art museum, did you?"

"I did." *She could almost smell the fluid oils as she and the director reviewed painting after painting. She had always cherished the fragrance of the palette, the velvet hues that clung and clung and could be removed from the fingers only with turpentine. What an enchanted day—being led past human history. Medieval religious canvases. Winged plump cherubs; the artist's patron drawn in miniature at the bottom of each ethereal scene. So whimsical! The stern real-people portraits of the Renaissance. The stirrings of modern art: thousands of dots meticulously placed to create a single mosaiclike scene. Everlasting beauty.*

"What happened?"

"They didn't need anyone."

"Oh."

"So much for that idea."

"Well, maybe they'll have an opening soon. It's hard to imagine that they'd pass you up."

What time was it? Thoughts of Leona and Kevin gripped her. "Look, I've got to get going."

His fingers found the side of her face; his thumb slipped under her chin to lift her mouth firmly to his. The insistent kiss brought a spreading ache to her. She had dreamed of this: a good person, to hold her and then be gone. Through the long five-year winter nothing had bloomed. Now here it all was—offered candidly, like a handful of daisies from a child.

"What do you want, Judy? Tell me." His desire was close. Inside her. Weaving along the secret passageways. Alive.

"You," she whispered. "I want you."

Saturday, October 14, 1972

"YOU DON'T have to tell me, I already know." Susan glanced up from the terrier she was grooming. "Who is it?"

Judy tried to compose her expression. Susan was a radar dish. She caught it all. It didn't have to be audible or visible. "What makes you say that? Wishful thinking?"

Susan combed tufts of terrier hair into high knots and clipped them deftly. It didn't seem like a reasonable method, but the dog's coat—so far—was evenly shorn. "It's as though you've had a transfusion. You look a lot stronger and happier. Here. Hold Clarabell's collar, will you? She jerks her head around when I cut near her ears."

Judy hooked her fingers through the strap. "I *am* stronger and happier."

"Never mind." Susan grinned. "I know you're not going to tell me. But I hope like heck this affair has made you drop the idea of divorcing Ron. That whole thing gave me the willies."

"Big Brother was going to kick my teeth in. Right?"

"No, just do a few root canals. Okay, baby. You're finished." Susan patted the dog's rump.

Judy released Clarabell's collar, and the terrier sprinted away.

"That's the last one." Susan sighed, surveying the clumps of dog hair strewn across newspapers in the living room. "Let's see," she said, getting up, "I'll roll all this. I did six of those critters today. Can you believe it? Well, *are* you?"

"Am I what?"

"Still thinking of divorcing Ron?"

"No."

"Good."

What would Susan say if she knew about the airport incident? She'd go bananas. She'd do the old "I told you so." All that bogeyman stuff was unfounded. *The government'll getcha if you don't watch out.* As if Judy were on a list somewhere.

Susan carefully folded the mat of newspaper and held it out in front of her.

"Do you want me to get you a paper bag?"

"No, I'll throw it right in the garbage can." Susan headed for the back door. "I'm glad for you. I really am."

"I feel like I'm on a carousel. We keep coming around to the same spot in the conversation."

Susan went outside. Judy could hear clattering. Then she was back. "You don't have to be so shy about it. I'm the one who suggested it, remember? I think it's super. It's the most sensible thing you've done. I just hope you picked the right person."

Susan was so blunt! So nosy. Judy felt a surge of loyalty to Campbell, a stabbing resentment of Susan. Campbell *was* the perfect person. "And what's your description of Mr. Right?"

"He keeps his mouth shut, and he doesn't overstay his welcome. Oh. I can tell he's got that sewed up," Susan acknowledged, studying Judy's brows and cheekbones.

What did she see there? Judy had tried not to register any reaction.

"Oops. I've screwed it up again. I'm making you mad."

Judy shrugged.

"Hey, that's not what I started out to do. I started out to give you some encouragement. You wanna help me wash the dogs? That's next. After I style them, I do the shampoo number and blow dry. We just have to get these turkeys one at a time and put them in the washtub downstairs. You wanna do it? Come on."

"You're a turkey yourself," Judy said, giving Susan a playful pinch on the upper arm.

"I know. Follow me." She clucked to Clarabell, who was wedged into a corner of the dining room, licking her behind, and Clarabell followed them down the cellar steps.

Dismal. Dank. A solitary fogged window sent cold light spilling across the concrete floor.

"She can get down, but she can't go up again," Susan observed. "I have to carry her. Because there aren't any backs on the stairs. She doesn't notice it on the way down, but it spooks her on the return trip." She pulled the string on a bulb and a metal laundry tub was illuminated. "Clarabell's the only one that likes to have a bath. Aren't you, girl?" She pressed the rubber stopper into its hole and turned on the spigots. "Here comes some friendly advice."

"Oh, Lord." Judy slumped against the whitewashed cement block wall.

"Listen up," Susan said pleasantly, hefting Clarabell into the water. "Just enjoy yourself. Don't think about anything. Don't overanalyze it. You've earned a break from this friggin' war. Cut out that guilt number you're doing on yourself—don't deny it, I know you are—and build yourself up a little. You've been a rag, an orphan. Now you look good. Don't kill it."

Guilt. Kill.

Ron. Hanging by his wrists. Christ-like. In agony.

Susan stopped soaping Clarabell, blinked at Judy sympathetically in the harsh brilliance. "Ronnie's coming home," she said. "You'll see. You have a solid marriage. Nothing's going to destroy that. He thinks of you, too. He's not saying to himself 'I have it rough, she has it easy.' He's saying, 'We both have it rough. But I'm going to make it. I hope she takes care of herself any way she can. I hope she makes it. That's all I'm asking. Just for the both of us to make it through.' Wouldn't you be saying that if you were Ron?"

Susan reached out and put a warm drop of soap suds on one of Judy's fingers. A mark of affection.

"You're making it, kiddo. Hold on."

Monday, October 16, 1972

"You FILTHY bitch." A woman's voice, over the telephone line. "Wait till your husband finds out what you've been up to."

About Joe? Who? "Who is this?"

"Don't hang up, sweetheart, I have something to tell you. I saw your picture in a magazine: glamour girl in New York City. How come they didn't show you kissing all those gooks on their skinny yellow asses?"

"Who *is* this?"

"You think you're getting away with it but—"

"I'm not trying to get away with anything. It's a free country. I have the right to my opinion, and I have the right to express it."

"Unless I miss my guess, you're about to get a red, white and blue fist down your throat."

"Judge me after you've been where I've been."

"I've been there. And I think I'm qualified to say that you're a first-class A-number-one shit."

There was a click like a bold black period at the end of a sentence. Judy slammed the telephone receiver down and whacked her fist against it. Damn, damn. It was starting again. The nightmare. The uncertainty. Why had she thought she could climb out?

Who was the woman with the razor-blade voice? Another POW wife? There had been a static hum in the background. Long distance?

The phone rang again. Shrill. Accusing. She walked away from it, over to the kitchen window. They had done a good job of replacing it. Would all the rest be fixed? Ever?

The phone continued to ring, piercing and angry. She snatched up the receiver.

"Yes!"

"Mrs. Greer?" A man, startled.

"I am."

"This is Duncan Crockett . . . at the museum."

"Oh. Hello."

"We were certainly impressed with . . . with you. We had budgeted for an additional person to come on next year. But now we want to go ahead, two months early. Do you follow me?"

"Not exactly."

"We want you to work for us, Mrs. Greer. Are you still interested?"

A gift. Her life in art. Her life. Who *she* was, apart from all the circumstances, the entangling relationships. Art.

"Mrs. Greer?"

"Oh, yes. I'd like that. Very much."

"How many weeks' notice do you need to give your present employer?"

"Two."

"Two weeks, then. Say, November first?"

CHAPTER *16*

Saturday, October 21, 1972

SHE DRIFTED awake, surprised to find a man's arms encircling her naked breasts, his knees drawn up under the backs of her thighs. Joe Campbell.

Judy stirred slightly, looking about in the darkness, trying to remember where they were. In his sleep Joe pushed a leg over hers.

A bedroom loft. His house . . . at the edge of a fallow cornfield.

The window beside them stretched all the way to the carpet, and moonlight illuminated the glaze of frost that had settled across the panes: a pattern of perfect snowflakes, crystal after shining crystal. The silence was complete. They were caught—timeless, peaceful—inside the starry ice.

She shifted as best she could in order to see him, tracing the sculpt of his head with her gaze. In the hours of their lovemaking she had come to learn each of the tiny lines beside his eyes, each of the few white hairs starting in his sideburns. He had even made her laugh! She marveled at it. Laughter, which had been frozen under her tongue and now was not.

She had explored him timidly, then with joy; the air was filled with the things they would not say. When it seemed at last they must speak to each other or weep, they had held their words and, thoroughly spent, slept.

It had all been as he had promised: a free island. No shame. There was nothing about him she did not like. Gratitude flowed in her, a deep tenderness for him.

His eyelids fluttered, and he, waking, focused on her face. "You all right?" he asked.

116

"Yes."

"What time is it?" He leaned up on one elbow, fumbling beside him for his watch.

"Can you see it?"

"It's got a fluorescent dial. Twenty minutes to four." He lay back, staring at the ceiling and then glancing around the room as if trying to recognize it. "Lord, Judy, I can't believe you're here with me." He reached for her, and she rested against his side, under the sensual weight of his arm. "You're not worrying, are you?"

"No."

"She'll never find out you weren't with Susan."

"I know." They existed in separate compartments, Joe and Leona. They could not overlap.

"I never thought this would happen, that you'd come here with me." He kissed her hair.

"How *did* you get me to do this?"

"I took a course in persuasion."

She laughed.

"That's what it was called: Persuasion. No kidding."

"A college course?"

"Yes. How to get people to do what you want them to do."

"Like what?"

"Anything." He sleepily propped himself up on the pillows. "I've got a good story from that class. Here was this really sober professor, giving us a lot of statistics and studies on how to persuade, and who persuaded whom of what, and when. Most of that sort of coercion is done without people knowing they're being influenced—subliminal suggestion. We decided to perform an experiment on the instructor."

"Without his consent."

"Right. Whenever he walked over to one side of the room, we'd give him our full attention, we'd look delighted with what he was saying."

Judy could imagine the rest. She giggled.

"On the other hand, when he went to the middle of the

room, we'd appear to lose interest, to be daydreaming. And when he moved clear over to the left . . ." Joe gestured.

"You acted like you didn't want to have anything to do with him." She rubbed her cheek against his shoulder, amused.

"That would have been too obvious. We acted confused, as if we couldn't understand the points he was making. It took the whole semester, but guess what."

"His zone got smaller!"

"And smaller! After a while he wouldn't go into the middle anymore—and never to the other side. He was stuck in a corner, for every lecture."

"An invisible leash! Did he ever find out?"

"Sure. That was part of it. We told him on the last day. We thought he'd call that the greatest experiment of all: persuading the Persuasion professor. But he was teed off. Didn't say anything, just packed up his briefcase and left the room. We were flogging ourselves for two weeks until the final grades came in. But he was fair about it."

"People don't like to be fooled."

"Surprised us about him, though. We didn't think he'd mind so much." He gripped her at the ribs and pulled her up onto his muscled torso.

Man. She hid her face in his neck. Beautiful night.

Ron.

No. Don't think about it. She straddled Joe's abdomen, sliding down, brushing her lips across his chest, letting her fingers seek the moist rapid breath of his mouth.

"Judy . . ." he whispered against her hand.

Wind began to cry along the peaks and eaves of the house, to whistle in the slender crack beneath the window sash.

Her lover. It almost seemed she had thought him up. The contours of his body and his life fitted so perfectly with hers. How could it have happened this way?

Her knees found his hips. An invitation. He pressed

himself gently into her; she shivered with pleasure, and he drew the warm blanket around her shoulders, kissing her, kissing her.

Now it would all begin again: the owning and the fierce delight. She had never before known sex without marriage. It had amazed, even disturbed her to understand the power of a purely sexual bond. The church labeled such a thing lust. But this physical adventure with Joe consisted of loyalty and affection—of overwhelming, demanding emotion which excluded all other people . . . all personal history, all futures.

What really made it different from love? And how long could it stay a separate thing?

Morning.

She scanned the loft. The sound of shower water touched her consciousness. He was in the bathroom.

This was her first daylight look at his rented farmhouse, the high, slanted ceiling and wooden beams. Sparse furnishings . . . bed, bookshelf, desk, dresser. It had the feel of a hotel room. Hardly any personal belongings.

There were two small pictures on the dresser, in a double frame. Young girls. Daughters? She got up, stung at once by the winter chill. He had left a blue terry robe on the end of the bed. She put it on. It was huge; she turned up the sleeves, wound the bulk of it around her.

Now she could see. The girls were mid-teens. The older one had Joe's green eyes and a familiar curve to her lips. Did they miss their father terribly?

She was so curious about Joe. He was not one to let his past surface in conversation—not the important parts of it anyway—and this loft had a distinct absence of personality. No old clippings or diplomas or awards. No letters, no bills accumulating on the desk top. Just a few sporting and outdoor magazines . . . a couple of recent best sellers. *The Godfather, QB VII*. Nothing definitive.

"Judy." She hadn't heard the shower stop, but here he

was, wrapped in a towel, hair wet. He came toward her, pressed her to him. He smelled good. Toothpaste and sweet soap.

"Are these your girls?" she asked, picking up the flowered silver frames.

"Yes. That's Joanne, she's sixteen. And Stephanie. Fifteen."

"Where do they live?"

"With their mother."

"I mean *where*?"

"Connecticut." He took the photos from her and set them back on the dresser.

"Do you see them very much?"

"Not as often as I'd like to."

"Is that where you were raised, Connecticut?"

"Part of the time." He tugged on the belt of her robe. "Come on, want to get your shower while I'm shaving? It's too cold to stand around like this."

"You don't want to talk about it."

"About?"

"Your children . . . your childhood, where you've been. Where you're going."

He considered her thoughtfully. "No."

"Why not?"

"There's an old saying—by Confucius: Life is really simple, but people insist on making it complicated."

What did he mean? She studied him, the kind eyes, the generous mouth, and put her arms around his neck for reassurance.

He embraced her. Warmly. Nothing had changed.

"Please," he whispered, his breath filling her ear. "Please, Judy."

Please what? How could she understand him?

"Let it be," he said.

Then she saw it.

For them to survive this affair without grief, they had to keep it on the simplest possible level. There were already shared memories piling up.

And pain was the only plausible ending. Parting.

"I wish Kevin were here," Judy said as she and Joe knelt on the living room rug, untangling the strings of two dingy kites he had found in the basement. "Kevin would go crazy for this."

"Well, let's bring him out here someday. He's a great kid. I like to be with him."

Judy smiled at Joe. "You do, don't you?"

"Amen. And that's going to be one red-hot game on the tenth. Kevin'll give 'em the Roaring Freight Train. He's got the stuff. You'll be a proud mama, wait and see."

"I am proud anyway."

"You're going to be prouder." Joe opened the door for her, and they inched down ice-slick steps onto his front lawn. The grass was hoary and stiff; icicles hung from the birdhouse.

November 10 game. Friday afternoon. That was the Veterans Day weekend; she'd be with Connie and the Vietnam vets in Washington for a protest. "I don't think I can get to that game. In fact, I know I can't."

"Why not?"

"Well, I'll be in Washington."

"For?"

"A march. Can't miss it." They trudged through a barrier of weeds onto black, rippling dirt.

"Yes. I guess they like it when you show up. You're one of the more notable faces. POW wife coming out against the war."

"And coming out and coming out and coming out. I wonder if it's doing any good."

"What do you think?"

"I think it has. But even if it hasn't, it's something I've got to do."

He seemed disturbed. He uncoiled the kite twine, testing it by pulling it taut between his hands.

"Do you want to lay it on me?"

He grinned. "Do I want to lay on you?"

She winked at him. "No . . . that's not what I said."

"Okay. Kevin needs you right now. It would cause a lot more trouble for you to go away on the weekend of possibly his most important game."

It was true. He would feel slighted. He had made it so clear.

"Am I right?" The wind was searing them now. They turned their collars up and snuggled into them.

"Probably. But I keep thinking that later on he'll understand what I did and why. It's really for him. It's for all of us. I can't quit trying to get this war stopped, trying to get Ron home again."

He touched her cheek. "Judy . . . do you believe in me?"

What a funny thing to ask. She raised her eyes and regarded his expression. Caring. Wise. She trusted him. "Yes. I do."

"Then listen. This is a critical time for Kevin. He needs you more than he ever has. Couldn't you, just once, put the war issue aside and let Kevin move up to number one? It would help him so much."

"He is number one."

"But he doesn't know it. Show him."

She thought of Connie. *You wouldn't back off, would you? We're going to win.*

"What's your top priority?" he said, bending down to kiss her lightly on the nose. "I can only do so much for him, Judy. I'm an outsider."

His mood changed. "If you're going to be director of the museum eventually, Mrs. Greer, you've got to master kite flying."

"A necessary skill," Judy agreed. "Hey, you don't even seem surprised that I got the job."

"Why should I be? You're overqualified. Kite flying: lesson one. Run!" He started along the stripped cornfield, letting string out little by little as his kite began to lift. He shouted something back to her, but the words scattered in the breeze; his hair stood straight out, waving wildly. The kite soared upward, and Joe began to move in a wide arc across the brittle soil.

A great day! Exhilaration rose in her like music. She sprinted away from him, into the wind, feeling the kite wrenched from her grasp and beginning to take its own direction.

The string slipped rapidly between her fingers; she came to the end of it and held on tightly while the kite tore at her, tried to snatch her from the ground. It made her think of eagles and unsuspecting mice, the childhood dream in which she—the mouse, terrified—was swept up over the plow marks. But with fear had come fascination with the receding patchwork earth, the hooking rivers. Curiosity. She would find the eagle's aerie—a nest so high that only doomed prey had access. She might be devoured, but she would see the Secret Place.

How many times in her girlhood bed had she been the mouse, darting beneath the shadow of the eagle, seeking a hollow log, thinking that she was outdistancing him and then—with only a slight whish for warning and a momentary prickle of talons—having no choice at last.

They were coming full circle, on a collision course. Laughing, she crashed into Joe, and they both fell; their kites wafted down to smack against forgotten heaps of dry stalks. He turned over on her then, eager—their thick coats in the way, making him work to reach her lips.

CHAPTER 17

Wednesday, October 25, 1972

WHAT A STUPID time to have a fire drill! They got only twenty-two minutes for lunch anyway. Now he'd have to inhale his sandwich to get to history class on time.

Kevin followed the other students back through the double doors and down the stairs into the school cafeteria. The kids made a beeline for the tables where their lunches, untouched, were still sitting.

"Bologna doesn't thrill me," Andy said, turning his chair around and mounting it as if it were a horse.

Justin and Sam also came to roost, and Kevin opened his carton of milk.

"Wouldn't you know today's special would be bologna," Sam griped. "I could have brought *that* from home and kept the money."

Kevin was famished. He took an oversize bite of the sandwich. Sesame seeds. Soft bun. Fancy or not, it tasted super. Wait a minute. He stopped chewing. It wasn't bologna, it was . . . *Oh, no. That's crazy.* He spit the bite into his napkin and looked at it.

"Gross," Justin said.

Kevin held the whole thing down by the side of the table and examined it. Paper. In his sandwich! He rolled the mess up. Wet. Disgusting. And laid it on the floor beside him.

All three boys were staring.

"What was it?" Justin asked.

"I don't know." He knew. He lifted the top off the remaining sandwich. The bologna was missing, and in its place, slicked with mustard, was a torn-up photo of his mother—the picture out of the damned newsmagazine.

"Holy cripe," said Andy. "Who did that?"

They looked around, but the other students all seemed to be talking or wolfing their meals. They had only about three minutes left on D lunch break.

"What're you going to do?" Sam asked. He seemed scared. Justin and Andy did, too.

Kevin shook his head. The picture had been shoved under his nose in some cruel way half a dozen times in less than a month. Once it was even on the toilet paper roll when he went to the boys' bathroom. At first he had been angry and vengeful, but that had subsided into a quiet loathing. For the kids? For his mother?

He didn't know who was after him. It didn't make any difference anyway—it wasn't these three; they all were wearing the bracelets and looking at him as if he were being electrocuted. "Eat," he said. "You've only got about two minutes."

"Here, we'll share." Andy started to tear his sandwich in half. "Oh, piss."

The boys followed his gaze. Pieces of a picture were falling out of the middle of Andy's sandwich onto the plate. Andy gestured at the other two, and they dissected their bread. Photos. Kevin's mother.

"Holy cripe." Andy again.

Sam took a swig of milk and choked on it. Kevin realized it was because he was laughing. How could he? Sam gulped, then cracked up some more.

"Did you do this, Sam?" Kevin demanded, instantly furious.

"Hell, no." Sam coughed. "I didn't do it. But they sure got us, didn't they?" The tears were coming now, and he wiped at his eyes with his sleeve. "Talk about biting on it! Chomp, chomp."

Andy had abandoned his scowl and seemed bemused by Sam's reaction.

I've made them into targets, Kevin thought. *Sucked them down with me.* Had they been getting the "photo treatment" recently, too?

"You been zapped before?"

"Shoot, yeah," Sam said. "They been stickin' it to us all month."

Kevin stiffened.

"But that's okay." Sam shrugged—a little too casually. His voice got louder. "We don't care, do we?"

Andy looked away.

Justin got up abruptly, jerked his tray from the table and walked off. Kevin flushed with embarrassment. These guys had been getting a dose of it. Photos crunched up in the toes of their gym shoes, no doubt. And substituted for stolen pages of their homework.

It killed him. He wanted to throw up. To die.

On the way back to class, as Kevin paused in the hallway for a drink of water, a kid waiting behind him—one whose name he didn't know—said slyly, "How did you like your lunch? It was *real* baloney today."

"Don't want any dinner?" his mother said, crossing in front of his bedroom TV to turn on a lamp and study his face.

"No, thanks."

"You've just been lying here watching cartoons? With the sound off?"

"Yeah. I feel like it."

"Are you sick?" She touched his forehead with cool fingers. "I'm going to get the thermometer and see if you have a fever. Do you hurt anywhere?"

"No." He kept his gaze on Daffy Duck, who was trying to avoid a lone cloud. It followed him closely, hovering over his head, dumping rain in sudden bursts.

"Kevin . . ." She sat next to him on the bed. "Do you want to talk?"

"No." He wished to heck she'd go out and close the door.

"Please," she said. "Can't you tell me? Is it something that happened at school?"

He left Daffy and checked her over. She looked so

pretty, so . . . in control these days. She'd got herself all changed around. Mostly.

She took his wrist and held it. "I'd like to know."

She should already know. The trouble she was getting him into. Baloney. All that baloney that she did. She should find out what happened today, how he almost ate her Technicolor head. But where would he get the words for that? It would crank her up.

"Is it about the kids at school?"

"Yeah." He rolled to the other side of the bed and put his face in a pillow.

There wasn't anything she could do. If there were a way out, she would have given it to him by now. She was unbending on this war thing. He had never seen the hint of a second thought in her.

Could she be right after all?

No. When you're right, you have lots of people around you. The things she did and said were despised.

Monday, October 30, 1972

Dear Judy,

What has changed? I know what you told me on the phone, but I can't believe it's you talking. I wish I could see you. There's something you're not saying. Why won't you come to Washington? We need you! I was so proud of you when that airport picture came out this month—you shouting a welcome to those poor devils. People know you. You're a symbol for this whole thing. Why back out now?

I know about Kevin. He deserves better. I know all that, but what about Ron? This is important. People will think it's over, and you know it's damned well not. I don't care what Kissinger says. That "peace is at hand" announcement—crap. Can't you get what they're trying to do? They'll love it that you finally shut up.

Okay—I know you said you'll come to the next one, but I don't get the good feelings about it. It's like you're hiding, and we used to be totally together.

Did Grant say something when you were here? He's not too good,

Judy—still having a lot of trouble. Whatever he did against you—if anything—I hope you will forgive. He has a good heart. Think of the four of us sailing Back When. Remember? Sun blisters and beer. He's just been wrapped around himself by what happened in Nam.

I am really sick about the election. I'm pretty sure our boy is going to lose. We've been busting our picks humping for McGovern, but there's a lot of sneaky things going on to get him beat. Believe me. Them that has keeps. (Tell you later.) Watch out behind you.

Well, it's 3:00 A.M., and I'm getting punchy. Write to me. Tell me what you are thinking about—really.

Here's a hug and X,
Connie

CHAPTER 18

Tuesday, October 31, 1972

ANDY HELD THE bracelet out to Kevin. "Here. I need to give this back to you." They were standing in front of their lockers in the school's front hallway. "Here, take it. Come on," Andy said glumly. "I have to get to class."

Kevin pretended he was looking for a pencil. He reshuffled the contents of the locker shelf.

"Come on, Kev. Kev?" Andy tucked the bracelet into the pocket of Kevin's slacks. "Look . . ." He tried to make eye contact. "I still want to be friends. I just think things would be a lot cooler if I didn't wear it, okay?"

Well, what did he expect? Some of them were going to fink out. And it was Halloween. That would probably bring a lot of hassle.

"All right," he muttered.

"What?" Andy leaned closer.

"I said *all right.*"

"You're not mad?"

"No." He hardly formed the word.

"What?" Andy said again.

"I'm *not* mad."

Andy closed his locker and spun the combo dial. "See you at lunch." He waited for a minute, then, receiving no answer, sauntered off down the hall.

Whang! Something hit the back of Kevin's locker and clattered onto a pile of books. *Another bracelet.*

Kevin glanced around in time to see Justin open the door to the stairwell. Justin didn't look back.

The overhead lights in the classroom seemed harsh and

made him squint. The room was ugly. Institution green. Every wall in the school was painted the same way. There were no comfortable surfaces here; they all were hard. The blackboard, tile floor, wooden seats. He couldn't concentrate. Mrs. Hanover's voice sounded tinny and far-away.

"Kevin, are you with us?"

He peered at her over the bobbing heads.

"Yes."

"Good." She went back to her description of a medieval fortress, zealously drawing turrets and moats across three boards.

The sky beyond the window was yet another wall: solid, mournful cloud cover. Low. Close. His legs tingled. He tried stamping them gently, stretching his feet back and forth. His ankle and knee and hip joints pulsed with confined energy. He needed to jump around; was itching to, aching to. But the room was static, the only action by Mrs. Hanover as she scrawled her way along. The only sounds were the scratching of chalk and an occasional murmur of pages.

Outside the silent glass, bare trees shook; twigs snapped and flew away. Hedges quivered as though they were about to be ripped from the ground. Stray pieces of paper and dead leaves hopped by, tumbled, hopped some more, careening out of sight.

Twenty-five minutes left in this period alone. He tightened the muscles of his back and shoulders, squeezed, let them hang loose on his skeleton. He had lasted this long—all morning and through lunch. Another couple of hours and the school day would be in the bag; he could go home.

Home. A box. Stuffy. Now the energy was humming in his ears, making him thirsty. Kevin chewed a corner of his mouth.

He wouldn't go . . . right away. He'd start off the other direction, hitchhike maybe, around I 465. Yeah. A car trip down under and to the west side of the city. Up over the top again and back home.

Or?

"Thanks," Kevin said. He slammed the door, stole a last look at the driver. Sort of a weirdie. A guy with an obvious hairpiece and not much to say.

The car took off, and Kevin stuck out his thumb again. It was cold as the dickens on the interstate. The traffic, at seventy miles an hour, stirred up one hell of a chill factor. Kevin walked backward slowly, his fist freezing. Anyway, it felt good. He had needed this for a long time—not to see anything familiar, to be cast into a world that did not know his name. The restless twinges in his legs had subsided.

A rusty turquoise Corvair passed him, then weaved off the pavement. Stopped. Kevin ran toward it. Old wreck! Unbelievable.

"Where are you headed?" the man asked when Kevin jumped in.

"Just . . . around the loop. Wherever you're going."

The man's eyes were red; his lids, fat and saggy. They matched the beefy face and a belly that pressed against the steering wheel. "Chicago."

Kevin was suddenly suspicious of this man. He had a sour odor.

But he wasn't going to back out. That would be silly. Sissy. This guy couldn't do anything. He could hardly move. Besides, the heater was on and Kevin's fingers were beginning to respond to the warmth.

"Sure." Why not?

The man released the emergency brake, puffing with the effort. The door beside Kevin opened. Someone grabbed him at his armpit and tried to yank him from the car.

Fear shot through Kevin's spine—a fountain, momentarily paralyzing him but injecting him with the instinct to fight.

"Get outta that car!" *Campbell*, his cheeks pink with anger, his body poised like a boxer's.

"Do you know this man?" the driver said.

"No."

"Get out!" Campbell barked, hauling Kevin across the seat. "Out!"

"Wait a minute . . . you can't . . ." The coach thought he owned Kevin. He didn't.

Campbell used both hands now to extract Kevin from the car.

"Is this your kid?" the driver asked, leaning forward as best he could to frown up at Campbell.

"No. Call the police," Kevin said, still struggling.

The man regarded Campbell for a minute and then sped away, the passenger door flapping. Kevin knew he was not going to call anyone.

"What the hell do you think you're doing?" Campbell seized Kevin by the jacket collar and propelled him toward the station wagon. "If I hadn't been out here, coming back from taking some full bird to the airport, you would have gone for a ride with that jerkimo! What's the deal?"

They had reached the wagon now. Campbell opened the door and tried to stuff Kevin in. Kevin resisted. Campbell locked his arms around Kevin's waist. They began to wrestle. Kevin broke free and ran toward the side of the road, where the grass fell steeply into a ravine.

"Give up." Campbell motioned at Kevin. "You're not gonna get away from me." They circled each other. "I'll knock you cold if I have to."

Another car pulled over, kicking up gravel. Kevin could see that the folks inside looked frightened.

"They think you're being kidnapped," Campbell said. "Is that what you want? Somebody's going to shoot me in a minute. Get in the damned car."

Kevin glanced again at the people, who evidently had decided that saving this boy was worth risking their lives. It was a middle-aged couple. They were climbing out of their car.

Kevin dropped his defense, waved them back. "It's okay," he shouted.

"Is he your father?" the woman called.

Kevin could go with them. They would take him home. He knew Campbell would not tangle with this pair, who were so white-faced, so appalled.

He hesitated for an instant, then yelled to them over the whine and thunder of the traffic. "It's all right. He's . . . a friend. A friend of mine."

"Don't give me any more of that yep-nope stuff." Campbell swung the car onto the post grounds. "I want to know what you're thinking about."

Tears moved up and down in Kevin's throat, clinging to his Adam's apple. "My mother makes me crazy."

"Come off it. Nobody makes us crazy. If you go crazy, you do it to yourself. Your mother and dad are both doing the best they can right now. They're in a lot of trouble, but they're being very brave. Now what about you?"

Trapped. Being in the car was like being inside an egg. The shell curved too near Kevin's face. He was growing larger, up against the windshield.

A bugle began to play "Retreat" over the post's loud-speaker system.

"Nuts." Campbell jammed on the brakes. All cars were stopping, their uniformed occupants jumping out to stand at attention, saluting. It happened every day at five o'clock.

Campbell got out. Kevin knew the coach was bound by post rules to remain at attention until the ceremony ended with a round of cannon fire and the lowering of the flag.

Take off.

Kevin worked the door latch and stumbled into a dead run. Campbell would come after him, but Kevin had a head start. A big one. He zigzagged between buildings, trying not only to cover distance but also to take as many unexpected turns as possible. The cannon fire came: noisy blank rounds that echoed in his chest.

He passed behind the movie theater and emerged at the firehouse. Should he head for the barracks area or out across the golf course? Golf course. Too many people in the company area to get in his way. The first few holes were in full view; he needed to run down the road several yards and go for the far greens.

The bugle piped "To the Colors" and faded. Pavement stung Kevin's feet. He could hear himself wheezing; he was really tired. He dug his heels into a grassy bank and pounded up onto the course. There were no players. Darkness filtered along its edges. He stayed on the diagonal, charging for the end of the links and the wilderness beyond: a woods where maneuvers were held. He could get lost in there.

Campbell materialized out of nowhere. A ghost, lunging for him, pursuing him as Kevin's fear took him swiftly into the trees.

"Kevin!"

He dared not look back.

"Please. Kevin. For Pete's sake."

The crunching and rustling as he leaped through the dry weeds seemed huge. *God! What was this? A fence. A goddamned chain-link fence.* He went up it like a monkey, reaching the top, feeling the barbed wire bite his fingers and Campbell pull his feet all in the same instant.

He fell, smashing into Campbell, jarring against the earth with such force that the scream in his mouth jolted away from him, leaving a hiss in its place.

Campbell knelt beside him, straining for breath. "I know what makes you run," he said sadly. "I know. You're in a cage . . . like your father."

"My dad's dead."

"He's not."

"How do you know?"

"He's alive. He's coming home. Soon."

"If he's alive, why doesn't he ever write to me?"

Heavy rain began. Campbell stood up. "Give me your hand."

Kevin knew what it meant.

"If you won't come out of the cage, at least let me in there with you."

"You'll leave me."

"Yes. I'll have to. But by that time you won't need me."

Kevin closed his eyes and lay for two or three minutes

with the cold rain pelting his face, rolling under his collar, drenching his hair. When he looked up again, Campbell was still in the same pose, but with both arms outstretched.

Kevin reached for him.

CHAPTER 19

Friday, November 3, 1972

"I'VE NEVER seen so many crucifixions," Susan said reverently, her voice echoing among the paintings and sculpture.

"For a long time Christianity was considered the only suitable subject for art."

Susan nodded, her hoop-link earrings jangling. "I'm really interested. I just don't know what I'm looking at. You'll have to tell me. By the way, there's a painting in the other room I think is upside down."

Judy gave Susan a wry glance and a smile. Susan was no dummy. Not on the worst of days.

"It is, Judy. I swear it."

"In the modern art room?"

"Yes."

"Okay, I'll have them turn it. How long have you been in here?"

"About an hour. I didn't want to disturb you. I thought I'd browse and then come see you. What do you do anyway?"

"Oh . . . catalog the paintings, arrange for special exhibits . . . handle gifts to the museum. Stuff like that. Did you like what you saw?"

"Yes, but there weren't any pictures of dogs. Only once in a while—in some of those old portraits of families. How come all those people look like they've just had bad news?"

Judy put an arm around Susan's shoulders, trying to get a grip on her through her fake-fur coat. They grinned at each other. "It was in vogue not to look too chipper."

"I get it. That used to be in vogue at your house."

Judy squeezed Susan hard.

"What a great idea this was, for you to find a job here. You love it, don't you? Come on, walk me out to my car. How come we didn't think of this before?"

"Yes, okay and I don't know."

"What's that?"

"The answers—to your three questions."

They wound through the museum chambers. It was like living under a well-stocked Christmas tree, Judy thought. Each item exquisitely wrapped. For her! Even the artists' names were colorful, festive. *Bruegel, Rubens, Dürer, Vermeer, Van Gogh.* Ribbons and lace.

"Why is it so quiet in here?" Susan asked. "People whisper. Is there a rule—like in libraries and in church—something everybody else knows and I don't?"

"No." Judy laughed. "You don't have to whisper. I guess we tend to because the artwork is so awesome, so ancient." They had reached the entrance now and faced each other.

"Don't go out. It's cold."

Fondness for Susan stirred in Judy. "I'm glad you came. Thanks."

"You know me. I'm the Queen of Questions. Got to find out everything, see everything. Can't help myself." She clasped Judy's wrists. "You look like a real person in here—all grown-up."

Silly Susan!

"You're not the Army's kid anymore, under their thumb, playing by their rules. You broke out."

"I was never theirs."

"But you've got distance now." Susan leaned earnestly toward Judy, her face alight with friendship. "It's good," she said. "And it's getting better. How do you feel?"

"Like . . . a real person."

"Keep going." Susan stepped into the revolving door. "That's a fantastic—" The rest of the sentence was chopped off by a swoosh, but Judy could see her pointing toward the "LOVE" statue out on the lawn, a huge sculpture in metal. Twice as high as a tall man. It consisted of the letters *LO* perched up on the letters *VE*. The *O* was tilted outward, on a diagonal.

Judy watched Susan walk toward her MG, where there were, no doubt, four or five terriers shredding the seats.

Sunday, November 5, 1972

LEONA SLID a piece of steak onto her fondue fork and glanced around the table at Judy and then at Kevin. "Have some more. We're celebrating! It's not every day Carol Lynn has a baby."

"I like this idea," Kevin said. "Having a birthday party right on the day that Heather's born. I wish I could see my cousin. What do new babies look like? Are they all scrunched up and red like everybody says?"

"Not always." Leona placed the fondue fork carefully into the sizzling pot of oil. "You were, I think, the best-looking of all the grandchildren when you were born— just as smooth and white as you could be. And a full head of hair. Sweet. Your daddy, he just collapsed into himself when he saw you."

Kevin seemed pleased but uneasy. He fiddled with his fork, checking the doneness of the meat.

"And so quiet," Leona went on. "None of that screaming business like some babies do. You seemed happy to be here. Didn't he, Judy?"

"You were adorable."

He peeked up shyly from his plate.

Oh, my son. How far we have come.

"Are we embarrassing you?" Leona refilled Judy's wine-glass and her own.

He dug into his baked potato. "I like to hear about it."

Kevin's birth. Judy's most vivid memories of Ron surrounded that golden time. She remembered cradling Kevin; how solid he felt in her arms. Not like a little girl at all, definitely a boy. If she hadn't known his sex, she would have guessed. *A little boy!* She remembered Ron holding Kevin, staring silently at him for minutes at a time.

Visions came to her, crisp as photographs: blue ribbons around the mailbox; the WELCOME KEVIN sign Ron had hung over the Port-a-Crib. Glad for a son? Judy sensed he would have been every bit as ecstatic for a daughter. He had gone to the eight Red Cross classes with her, learning how to bathe and feed baby dolls. He set about with fatherly pride to change even the messiest of diapers, to wash the tiny, squirming body in the bathroom sink, crooning to the child, kissing the soft spot on the top of his head. In the middle of the night, when Kevin cried, Ron got up eagerly and brought him to their bed, where Kevin lay contentedly between them, sucking milk from Judy's breast. A circle of eternal devotion: mother, father, child.

"You're going to help Aunt Carol Lynn?" Kevin asked.

"I am. They'll be bringing her home from the hospital Wednesday."

Leona's moment to shine. Grandchildren were her specialty. Judy silently blessed Carol Lynn for wanting to have her mother there, for asking her to come all the way to Texas, wanting to share. That would be like Ron's sister. They were out of the same mold, all of Leona's children: pure in the mind, kind in the heart. She had to give Leona credit. Surely Nugget wasn't the main force behind the shaping of their sons and daughters. He had been too busy, seldom present.

"I can't believe how fast they bring new mothers home. When I had my babies, I was in the hospital at least two weeks." Leona began picking up their plates. "You sit there now. I have a surprise." She went past the swinging door into the kitchen.

"I guess you'll be gone, too," Kevin said tentatively.

"Where?"

"Washington."

"Kevin . . . I changed my mind. I want to stay here, to come to your game."

He sat up straight. "You do?"

"Yes. I want to be with you. I'd rather be with you."

He looked at her in amazement and gratitude, then seemed to realize the openness of his expression. He composed his gaze and stared down at the silverware.

"Happy birthday to you, happy birthday to you," Leona sang, marching in slow steps from the kitchen, carrying a pink-and-white cake ringed with candles. She tilted it slightly, and they could see the name Heather written among the sugary roses.

Kevin and Judy joined in, loudly.

Kevin. Angel. In the dancing candlelight he seemed to be moving toward her. Leona set the cake in front of him, and he stood, bending over it to make a wish. *Precious person,* hers and Ron's. She must guard him, keep him safe. *I've been confused, but I'll do better. Little boy. Ours.* He was part of Ron—the only part she might ever touch again. Her eggs slipped monthly away from her. And each one had a face. Each one was a baby. Their children, whom she would never see. What would they have been like, the lost ones? She mourned for them.

Kevin blew out the candles and sat down again, his cheeks flushed. Leona rotated the cake, deftly removing the candles, cutting large, gooey slices. "I guess we'll have to get someone to stay with you, though, Kevin," she said, wiping icing from her fingers with a napkin.

Kevin glanced up at Judy, blinking.

"Mom will be here."

Wednesday, November 8, 1972

"THE STAR-SPANGLED Banner" played softly in the darkness, interspersed with static.

What? She raised her head.

Good morning, the announcer said. *Election results are definite now: Richard Milhous Nixon, the thirty-seventh Presi-*

dent of the United States, has won a second term in office, defeating challenger George McGovern by a significant margin.

Drat. Damn! It was over, final. Judy flicked the knob on the clock radio. Connie must be furious. She would have been up all night in the McGovern headquarters; she'd be crying.

God. How could this happen? Weren't people sick of the war? Why would they buy into Nixon again? Was the whole thing rigged?

That was ridiculous—Connie's paranoia. There was no way in the United States of America that any group of people could rig a presidential election or even slant it.

She was partly to blame for this frightening event. She had slacked off—not just about the Veterans Day rally but before that. She hadn't rolled up her sleeves for McGovern. She had ignored Connie's pleas to help thwart Nixon in the early days of his campaign. Connie and others had even stood the expense of flying to L.A. in September to instigate a protest outside Nixon's $1,000-a-plate fund-raising dinner. Wherever he—and the war—could have been stopped, Connie had appeared, Connie had worked.

But who would dream he could win again? Didn't the people see? And Ron . . . Now she would miss the next step, the veterans' rally. She was bowing out. Gradually. *Why?*

Kevin. She had almost let him go down the drain. She had been looking at the overall picture and ignoring her own situation. It couldn't continue. What good was bringing Ron home if the family were gone, broken?

The way Kevin had looked at her when she said she'd stay with him! How could she go back on that?

CHAPTER 20

Friday, November 10, 1972

KEVIN FOUND his spot at the fifty-yard line and glanced over at the coach. Sweat was running off Campbell's forehead. In forty-degree weather! He signaled Kevin to shift back slightly.

What a choke: the other team five points up with practically no time left, no chance. If they could pull it out some way, they'd be city champs hands down. With only two games left and a near-perfect record, nobody could beat them for the title.

The ball was snapped.

Same dumb game. It didn't matter where Kevin headed, Justin wasn't about to throw the ball to him. Time after time he had been in the open, waiting for Justin's pass. The quarterback would draw his arm high, ball poised, while his eyes found Kevin, then scanned past him, trying to locate another receiver. Finally, one would show up, and Kevin would remain a spectator.

Well, if they were down on their luck, it was Justin's fault. At half time the coach had only skimmed the situation with a short comment to Justin: "Release the ball faster." Why did Campbell keep Kevin in? The whole team felt the tension. He was the problem, standing out there waiting goalside with his thumb in his navel. He felt like an ass.

Now gold shirts were pursuing Justin all over the field. Every few seconds he'd turn and look back to see who was open. He was about to eat dirt, with three hulks getting ready to mow him under. Miraculously Kevin was in the clear, close to the thirty-yard line. Justin backpedaled, searching, searching.

Kevin was it. The only choice.

Justin let the ball fly as he fell. Kevin edged back two or three yards and caught it easily. It felt funny in his hands—cold as steel. Was this the first time he'd touched it in this game?

He exploded into motion. From the corner of his eye he could see two defenders slammed down by his teammates.

But someone was behind him. He could hear the chonk-chonk of cleats on turf. Rats. He moved it a little faster, almost there.

Ak! His hips twisted with the weight of a tackle. He struggled to stay on his feet, dragging the guy a couple of more yards. Another body piled on, and Kevin staggered sideways. His shoulder hit the ground with such force that the ball popped from under his arm as though it had been fired. Sam dived on top of it.

Freaky, the whole thing was in slo-mo like part of a movie, the first time he had experienced such a sensation. He could see the gradual crinkle of Sam's grimace, could even zero in on the adhesive tape around the first finger of Sam's left hand. Chunks of grass floated up in all directions as other players slid onto Sam, twirled down quietly, bouncing.

They got up. The scoreboard clock had stopped at twelve seconds. Four-yard line. Kevin crowded into the huddle. Why wasn't Campbell calling time-out? He was the one who knew how this ought to be set up. But he was pacing in front of the bench, drinking a Coke.

Justin called the play: clean shot, up the middle, quarterback keeper. As they left the huddle, Justin gave Kevin a pat on the rump.

Why was life so sticky? You never knew who was really your friend. Maybe it never did get resolved; maybe you just went from day to day traveling toward each other, never quite getting there.

They crouched at the line of scrimmage. On this kind of play it was a flat-out battle of muscle, locking horns like rams. They had to leave about a foot and a half corridor into the end zone, tilting their men slightly off center with the first block.

He waited. A strange sensation crossed his neck; a surge inside him. *His mother. Campbell.* Their hope for him. Belief.

His man lunged at him. Kevin had been distracted, and now the opponent was a second or two ahead. No! Kevin sprang forward, loosing a well of unfamiliar strength. *She loved him.* They crashed helmets, Kevin sensing the superiority of his own will. Struggling, the boy tipped ... tipped. Enough!

Justin bulled through.

All right! Kevin jumped, punching the air. People flooded onto the field, throwing paper cups, leaping at the players, jubilant. Wails of victory came from their mouths in almost visible strands, then fragmented, fluttered up. Skyward.

His teammates were tussling playfully with Justin, trying to heft him onto their shoulders. A shadow overtook Justin's expression as Kevin ran toward him. Dislike? Sadness?

Apology? Yes, that was the closest.

The boys were doing a pretty good job of boosting Justin, but he kept slipping to one side.

Kevin shoved a shoulder under Justin's thigh and helped raise him.

Judy closed her bedroom door and stepped away from the mirror which hung on the back of it. The dress was exquisite: a full-length gown of off-white shantung, trimmed at the neckline in jeweled braid.

A new dress! It had cost $90, a fortune. She had wandered among the designer racks of Block's department store, seized by an urge to buy a splendid outfit, to adorn herself. She had not felt this way in a very long time, pride in her body, pleasure when she looked at her own face. Discovery. She was still there. And not that old either.

She lifted her gaze from the dress to her hair, which had

been cut and styled, much shorter. She held up her manicured fingernails with their subtle melon polish. Sugared Fruit. That's what the manicurist had called the shade.

Nostalgia mingled with appreciation as she regarded her whole self. She had returned, magically, to her own life. In preceding months—years?—her physical being had become merely an instrument, a vehicle to get her from one place to another, to communicate, to produce a token amount of work. She had kept it clean and reasonably dressed, but it had been lifeless, anesthetized. She had been taking care of an unresponsive doll whose only movement was the click of its eyelids, open-shut-open.

She looked beyond herself at the rows of Chinese books. The titles seemed the same in mirror image. What was the difference? It was all unreadable, unknowable. Where had he gone, the person who knew the answers?

She turned from the mirror as if to find him there, standing next to his belongings.

This was a strange ritual, her annual attendance at the Military Ball, a rite of voodoo, an exorcism. She was no more military than the pope was Buddhist. But she went. She liked the swivel of heads as she entered the room. An infidel among them! Their complacency was defiled. She stood for peace—not necessarily their touted "peace with honor," but peace at any price.

They had to invite her. It was protocol. It tickled her to think how their book of rules—always painstakingly followed, even at the cost of common sense—decreed that she should be in their midst. A POW wife must be both invited and officially escorted. Period.

She had gone every year, noting with satisfaction their increasing discomfort: the officers in their slick dress blues, obliged to fill her dance card, to initiate polite conversation.

The doorbell rang. Pity the poor escort! Probably drew the shortest straw. *Sorry, kid. The booby prize is five hours with a flaming liberal.*

She picked up her wrap, made a last mental check of

window locks and light switches, people: Leona safely with Carol Lynn, Kevin over at Sam's for the night.

The bell rang again.

Impatient rascal! Maybe they'd picked someone this year who was a match for her indignation.

"Look, I've gotta have a weed," Sam said to Kevin. They were sitting on the floor next to Sam's bed, listening to records.

"You're kidding."

"I'm having a nicotine fit."

Kevin regarded Sam cautiously. Was it a joke?

"You ever tried it?"

"No."

Sam motioned for him to be quiet. He checked the hallway, locked the door, pointed toward his bathroom.

They cloistered themselves inside it, and Kevin sat on the commode lid, nervously watching Sam unscrew the top of an old deodorant jar.

"That's my ashtray. Then I flush them down." He pried open a Band-Aid tin and pulled out a pack of Marlboros complete with matches.

"It's not grass, is it?"

Sam offered him one. "Just a regular ol' coffin nail."

Kevin took it awkwardly, examined the filter, the tobacco end.

"Lucky I have my own bathroom, huh? But it's too cold to blow the smoke out the window. We'll have to use Plan Two."

Kevin was dazzled, intrigued. He had a friend. With whom he could spend the night, share secrets. He couldn't remember sleeping over with anyone else.

Sam had a great sense of humor. Even his appearance was slightly comical. His eyebrows slanted upward in diagonal lines from the bridge of his nose, which gave him a look of continual surprise. His hair was a bushy mop of tight blond curls, like a clown's wig. But he never seemed to mind anything about himself. People weren't inclined to rag him because he usually laughed it off.

"What's Plan Two?"

"We lie on the floor, with our heads in the towel closet, and blow the smoke down the clothes chute."

They collected their equipment and got down on the black and white ceramic tiles. Sam lit a match, held it out to Kevin.

Kevin stuck the filter between his front teeth, in the middle. Sam put the match to the tip of the cigarette; Kevin watched it, cross-eyed.

"You have to suck," Sam said.

Kevin pulled air in through the cigarette. A hot blast hit the back of his throat. He gagged, almost dropping the fool thing. Sam, as a reminder, pushed Kevin's head toward the open chute in the bottom of the closet. Kevin released the nasty taste—burned leaves, medicine—and jerked upward for some fresh air.

"Like this." Sam took a smooth drag. The ashes glowed red. He shoved his head far down the chute and exhaled, came up smiling.

"Okay." Kevin was embarrassed that he had placed the cigarette at the center of his lips. An amateur. This time he imitated Sam, applying the filter resolutely to the side. But he didn't want that yuck in his lungs. He'd just take a mouthful and let it go.

He hung his head down the chute.

"Don't drop the ashes," Sam said. "Put them in here." He tapped his cigarette on the edge of the jar. Kevin did the same. They looked at each other in triumph.

Sam took a deep breath of smoke and forced it out his nose, slowly. Kevin was thoroughly entertained.

"Jeez, I forgot to blow it down the hole. Well, we'll air out before we leave."

It didn't taste that good. Kevin's tongue felt the way it did after he'd been throwing up, kind of scratchy-dry with some real tart juices bubbling up under it.

Sam stretched out on his stomach, over the chute, and took another puff.

"Sam, answer me. Sam!" Mr. Owens. There was a loud pounding at Sam's bedroom door.

"Sam—your dad!"

Sam came up, wide-eyed, chalky. "I dropped it."

"What?"

"Down the chute."

They leaped up, instinctively doing separate tasks, slapping the lid back on the jar, replacing the cigarettes in the Band-Aid can, cramming them into the sink cabinet, opening the window and fanning at it with the bath mat.

They hurried into the bedroom.

"Sam!"

Kevin ran over and sat on the end of the bed, pretending to look at albums.

"Sorry, Dad. We'll be right there."

He rotated the key, pulled the knob.

Mr. Owens peered in suspiciously. "You don't have to lock it. We'll give you all the privacy you want. You reading girlie magazines or what?"

"No, Pop."

He studied his son's face. "Everything okay?"

Kevin nodded. So did Sam—but the skin right under his nose looked green-yellow.

"Dinner in five minutes."

"Bring that tray out of our room, will you, Jim?" Mrs. Owens called. Sam's father walked away.

Kevin and Sam bolted down the two flights to the basement, luckily passing no one. The chute's receptacle was a large square pen ringed with chicken wire. Any minute now it would be in flames.

There was a small gate at one side, for pulling out the dirty laundry. They grabbed handfuls of cloth, throwing slacks and pajamas into a pile on the cement; blouses, sheets, linen napkins. Must be the day before washday! They were frantic, yanking and tossing—but carefully. Watching.

The cigarette flew out of a red tangle: Sam's football shirt, a triangular hole in it still smoldering. Sam jumped onto the patch, stood on it, lifting his foot cautiously to see if the fire had gone out. Kevin stamped the cigarette dead and jammed it into his pocket.

Their eyes met.

They fell into the heap of laundry, laughing, burying their faces, snorting.

"Dinner, boys." Mrs. Owens. Upstairs. But she couldn't see them from where she was. It would be all right.

"Coming!"

They weakly crawled over to the chute and began stuffing everything back in.

"I'll hide the shirt behind the furnace," Sam whispered.

A mess. Sam would have to get it fixed some way. This was one of the most idiotic things Kevin had ever done—one of the craziest days he had ever had.

One of the best.

CHAPTER *21*

Donna Wellington tapped her husband's arm. "Here comes Judy Greer."

Tom glanced up from the Military Ball program he had been reading. Judy was approaching the post commander's table, escorted by Major Joe Campbell.

"She looks fantastic."

Tom nodded, watching her. She carried herself regally. A princess. Her gown was long and white and glittered at the throat. Major Campbell was holding her chair for her; she sat down gracefully. Tom noticed that most people nearby had paused to stare.

"She must be feeling a lot better," Donna said, leaning toward her husband to ensure the privacy of their conversation.

"She does. She told me."

"I'm glad. What do you suppose helped her out of it?"

Tom shrugged, baffled. "Don't know. Maybe the counseling, maybe the new job. Maybe she finally believes it's almost over. The waiting. With Nixon in again, it's sure to end soon. Thank God we don't have to backtrack and negotiate through another President. That could take forever."

"Her escort's handsome."

"That's Joe Campbell—TDY out of Washington."

"She doesn't look too comfortable with him."

"Why do you say that?" Tom crushed out his cigarette in a glass ashtray.

"I can just tell. She's not looking at him or speaking to him at all. It's as though he isn't there. He doesn't seem too pleased either."

"He didn't want to do it."

"Be the escort?"

"The commander talked him into it. There weren't many possibilities for her this year—single, the right rank and so on. He was the most logical candidate.

"Maybe he doesn't like her politics. General principles."

"Maybe."

Everyone else had left the table, to dance.

"Relax. Have a good time," Joe said quietly to Judy. "No one knows."

But she still felt upset with him. "I don't like surprises."

"Well, it was a surprise to me, too. I didn't know they were going to insist on my being your escort. Now I'm glad they did. You look . . . beautiful."

She glanced into the sincerity of his expression, then out at the dancers.

"Okay, I should have told you sooner. But I thought you'd think it was funny."

"I don't. Why couldn't you say no?"

"You can't tell the Army no. You follow orders."

True. The army was constructed of absolute obedience, pyramid-fashion.

He smiled. "Don't you know the old story about the bugler?"

Judy shook her head.

"It's almost a legend. On the day after a snowfall at Arlington a bugler was assigned to play 'Taps' for an Army funeral. He was to precede the cortege over a hill and down to the grave site, next to some woods. In the woods was another bugler. They were going to play echo 'Taps.' You know, one would play a few notes, and the other would answer. Well . . . the bugler who was stationed near the grave was told these orders: 'When the coffin passes you, start playing.' So he stood out there, waiting."

She raised her eyebrows at him.

"When the funeral party began to come over the hill, the coffin was first, carried by military pallbearers. The family was still on the other side of the crest. One of the pallbearers slipped on the ice and dropped the casket. The other pallbearers felt it wrenched from their hands and let go, too. The casket started downhill like a toboggan, gathering steam, heading for the poor bugler, who happened to be facing the other way and didn't see it coming. The casket slammed into the bugler, knocking his feet out from under him, breaking his leg and sending him—smack—into the snow. The coffin continued toward the open grave and, amazingly, went right over the hole and fell in. You're a military wife—what happened next?"

Judy, won over to him, laughed. "What?"

"The bugler, crying in agony from his broken leg, lifted the bugle to his lips . . ."

". . . and played 'Taps.' "

Campbell shrugged. "The coffin had passed. He had his orders."

"I don't believe it."

"That's the difference between us. I do. That's how it is."

The dancers floated past, and beyond them, dozens of tables dotted the room. Hundreds of dress blue uniforms. Thousands of combat ribbons, medals and gold braid. Over it all, the largest American flag Judy had ever seen was pinned high and flat to the wall above the stage, dominating the event.

"Hey . . ." He pinched her wrist. "It'll be okay."

What was she afraid of? That they would be discovered? At what cost? That Ron would abandon her? Perhaps.

No. What then? *Give it a name.*

The Army machine . . . its faceless judgment, its fervent backing of Ron. Would they hurt her if they knew about her affair with Joe? Would they? She thought of New York and the man with the watch.

No. They would not do more than hassle her, try to bring her into line. Her well-being was vital to Ron's emotional and professional future.

With an involuntary clamping of her teeth, she understood exactly why she was afraid.

The Army would hurt Joe Campbell.

If he got in the way.

Kevin hadn't realized it was a slumber party, but Justin Helms and Andy Warner and Jerry O'Toole—and two other guys Kevin didn't know—were dropping their sleeping bags onto Sam's living room floor.

"My neighbors," Sam said by way of introduction, "Craig Lenahan and Ray Farmer."

Kevin nodded at them.

"Sorry we're late," Jerry said. "We went to The Tank."

"What's that?" Kevin asked.

"This restaurant out by the Ohio line. All-you-can-eat seafood. It's a riot in there. You sit on tractor seats nailed to stumps."

"And they try to keep you from eating a whole lot by hanging gruesome stuff on the walls," Craig inserted. "Toilet seats and a half-open coffin with a bloody leg showing. And signs. Like . . . IT'S BEEN A GOOD DAY; NOBODY'S THROWED UP YET."

The boys spread out all over the carpet, comparing stories of food pilfering at The Tank—trying to get back outside with lobsters under their shirts. Kevin ended up next to Ray, who was quietly checking him out.

"You the one whose dad is a prisoner?" he asked.

"Prisoner of war." Why did people always have to bring it up?

"You sure he's alive?" Ray probed. He just seemed to want to know; he didn't seem to be trying to get Kevin's goat.

"We're not sure."

"When will you know?"

"I guess when the war's over and everyone comes home. And if he doesn't come . . . that's it."

Ray thought it over and offered sympathetically, "Well, you can always get a new dad. We got a new dad. After our old one left."

A new dad! There was only one real dad. The one who put the life in you. And when he was gone for good, that was the end of it. Anyone knew that. Dads weren't . . . *lobsters* . . . all pretty much alike.

"It's not terrible," Ray added, perceiving his dismay. "My new dad's nice. I helped pick him. We all did. Don't you know anybody you'd pick?"

"No." The suggestion agitated Kevin.

Then he thought of Campbell.

Judy tried to keep a little distance from her inebriated dance partner, a Colonel Swope—just back from Nam. She held her spine straight and her arms stiff, but he seemed not to notice. He hummed in her ear and crushed her to him as the tempo of the music picked up.

"You'll have to forgive the lack of conversation," the colonel apologized, missing several steps and bringing Judy around sharply to stumble over his shoes. "I'm in mourning."

"You are?"

"Damned right. For the South Vietnamese. Tricky Dick doesn't think we can win. I was told to come home. They're going to wind it up real fast now."

"I hope so."

He looked coldly into her eyes. "You don't know what you're saying, lady. It's going to be a massacre. As soon as the last GI climbs into his chopper, the executions will start. We're leaving those people out there with no defense."

"They have an army. We don't belong there."

"Where the hell are you getting your information?" His forehead wrinkled; all the veins stood out. He burped. Whiskey. "They're paper dolls without us. Cardboard. And the enemy's bigger than anyone's letting on. What's your name again, little lady? I'll have to remember your ignorance."

The song was ending. Thank heaven. "Judy Greer," she said.

His eyes narrowed. "Oh, shit, yes. You're the POW wife. I forgot it for a minute. Ron Greer. That your husband? Greer?"

"Yes."

"Well, you don't have to worry. They'll get *him* out. He's the expert on China, isn't he?"

"Yes." The final note of music sounded, and they stopped dancing.

"They'd never let that one fall through the cracks."

Kevin only dozed, periodically waking to the dark silence and unfamiliarity of Sam's house. He floated just under the surface of consciousness, losing touch, then remembering where he was, listening to others stirring and snoring in their sleeping bags. It astonished and thrilled him to be out of his own home, one of seven boys lined up across the living room floor, indistinguishable from the others. Just another kid! Accepted.

"So what?" he heard Justin whisper. The sound crackled in his ears, jolting him awake.

"So you promised. That's what." Sam's voice.

"I can do what I want."

"You already did. How come you and Andy had to chicken out on wearing the bracelets? We all were supposed to stick together."

Kevin felt a spreading heat under the top of his bag. He lay very still.

"I didn't like catchin' it, all right? I got sick of it. So did Andy."

"You turdball," said Sam. "That's how *he* feels every day."

"I'm afraid they'll hurt you, Joe."

"Who?"

They were lying in her bed, belly to belly.

"The Army."

"What do you mean? Why would they do that?" He shifted so that he could see her face in the light of the streetlamp.

She sat up. "If they find out about us."

"Why would they care?"

"Ron's a one-of-a-kind. They'll do anything they need to, for his security."

"Like keeping the family intact?" Judy thought he might laugh at her, but he rolled onto his stomach and put his head in his hands. "That makes sense."

She stretched out beside him, shaken. "You see it then?"

"They're not going to do anything physical to me. Is that what you think? That's nonsense."

"Is it? If you're in the way?"

"I'll get *out* of the way. I told you that."

"But what if *they* don't know that?"

"They're not going to do anything to me. This isn't Nazi Germany."

Spooked, she got up and crossed the room to the window, where she parted the curtains slightly. The street below was quiet, no cars. For a long time she studied the swaying patches of shadow beneath each tree.

Joe came over and stood behind her with his hands on her shoulders. "In the movies there's always some guy out there, some hit man smoking a cigarette, waiting for the right time. He knows what he's got to do." Joe lowered his voice and slowly walked his fingers up her neck. "After a while we'll hear him on the stairs. We'll try to call the police, but the phone will be dead. Uh!" He spun her away from the window. "Look! The doorknob! It's turning!"

She slapped him playfully in the chest.

He grabbed her hand. "Shhh! The door . . . it's opening. I can see the muzzle of a gun. BANG!" He lifted her unexpectedly, holding her high against him, nuzzling her breasts, growling.

She laughed. "Are you ever serious?"

"Not if I can help it." He staggered to the bed and fell comically onto her. She laced her fingers in his hair and guided his mouth down to hers.

He had looked at her all evening with admiration and a gentle possessiveness. For weeks she had sensed in him a turbulent, growing depth of emotion in spite of his casual veneer, his buoyant style. His way of caressing her had altered gradually, through a series of stages, as though they had moved toward commitment; he lingered over her body, hungrily breathing the breath of her, pressing her close to his heart.

And she? Loved him. Oh, yes, there it was. Loved him.

He put an arm beneath her waist; his knee touched the inside of her thigh. Tears began to slide from the corners of her eyes. Many tears. He felt the wetness in his own lashes and drew his lips away from hers.

"What is it?"

"I love you."

He sighed sharply. "Don't say that."

"I do, I do." She was crying, shuddering.

"You love your husband." It was half question, half statement.

"Yes."

"Don't start this."

"I love you and you love me. Say it." She wept.

"Judy! No."

But he took her. He didn't have to say it; it was all there in the deliberate, anguished intent of his body. She raised her knees up along his ribs, cradling him, meeting his urgent sorrowful passion.

"Damn it, Joe Campbell. Don't you ever cry?" she whispered fiercely.

"I can't." The words were broken, faint. He trembled in her arms.

She paused, on the sheerest edge of her desire, suspended, waiting for his lead.

He began. They were rushing toward each other in a very dark place, combining, grasping, spinning, rushing side by side through a midnight tunnel as streaks of yellow fire sped by. There was strong wind and the smell of rain and the protest of trees leaning in an awesome storm. They could not see where they were going.

And then they lost hold of each other.

CHAPTER 22

Saturday, November 18, 1972

"LET'S NOT stay too much longer." Campbell looked toward the amber lamps of the farmhouse. "Your mom's making a big apple pie. I don't want to miss out on that."

"Neither do I," Kevin said. "Just show me a few more stars. You can really see them in the country. How come you live way out here? It's lonely."

"I like my privacy. Not enough quarters on post for everybody anyway. You don't live there either, remember?"

"We get a housing allotment."

"Me, too, chief." Campbell swung the telescope in a different direction. The telescope wasn't what Kevin imagined it would be; not long and skinny. It was short and wide like a wastebasket, and with it you could see the rings of Saturn and the moons of Jupiter.

Campbell seemed to know everything about the heavens. He had recounted the myths of the twelve constellations in the zodiac, explained how stars were created—of cosmic gas—and how they eventually died, collapsing in upon themselves in a rush of violent self-destruction, churning into black holes.

The night was frigid and still. No blade stirred against another; no nighttime animal crept by in the thickets. The contours of earth were defined only by shades of deepest black, charcoal and gray. In all the star-dome arena there were only two touches of color: red curtains behind the glowing farmhouse glass.

Campbell locked the telescope into position and engaged the power drive, to track the star. "Kevin, I want to say something to you while we're alone."

His tone made Kevin touch the scope lightly to steady himself.

"Your father's coming home soon. Very soon now. And I'll be going away. I may not be able to come and tell you good-bye because ... when it happens, it will happen suddenly. Your father will be here, and I won't. Can you understand me?"

"But why do you think you'll be gone when my father gets home? I want my father to meet you."

Campbell looked down into the telescope's eyepiece, rotating the focus wheel. "The belt of Orion," he said. "Three stars in a row. From where we stand"—he pointed into the night sky—"they seem equidistant from one another. It's the belt of the Hunter. Remember I told you about the Hunter?"

Kevin knew from the way he spoke that it was so; he would be going away.

Forever?

"If you leave, I'll come to where you are," Kevin said. "I want to stay friends."

Campbell turned to him, but his expression was lost in the darkness. "I want to stay friends, too. Don't ever think we're not friends just because we don't see each other." His voice sounded as if it had rain in it. Water that he was trying to swallow. "Do you think your father loves you less because he doesn't see you?"

"I don't know."

"He loves you the same."

"But will he still love my mother? It could all be different."

"They love each other," Campbell said. "Believe that. Here." He peered into the scope's site again. "I want to show you a star. Mintaka. It's the top one in the belt."

Kevin moved closer. "How can you be so sure of everything? How can you even know if my father's still there?"

Campbell didn't answer.

"I wish you were my father."

Campbell's head came up quickly from the scope. "I'm not. I'm not your father. I never will be your father. I'm your friend. You have a wonderful dad, and he's coming home."

Kevin reflexively tilted his chin up. The three stars, one above the other, pulsed and winked.

"The top star is Mintaka. Now look at it in the scope."

Kevin closed one eye and put the other to the finder. "Which one is it?"

"That one," Campbell said.

"I know, but . . . I see two stars."

"That's it. That's Mintaka."

"Which *one*?" He glanced up at Campbell, puzzled.

"Both."

"You mean it's two stars?"

"A binary."

"It looks like one when you . . ."

"Two stars, orbiting a single center of gravity. Just because you can't see something doesn't mean it isn't there."

Kevin blinked at him.

"There's a whole lot we don't see. But we can believe in it anyway. Because we know it. We *know* it. Inside."

Kevin felt it then, too . . . tingling . . . the way he used to feel it in the beginning: his father's life. Real. Burning.

He traveled in an instant through a great, curved distance to the side of the bamboo cage; only this time it was not flat and movielike, but three-dimensional, each yellow filament round and shining. From the marshy, shrouded interior came a beam of rainbow crystals, filling him with anticipation and lifting him slowly, slowly, onto the top. Now he could see through the roof slats a gleam of hair and the intent angle of a man's head as he, silver-eyed, stared up at the constant stars.

Monday, November 20, 1972

HE WAS ROLLING down a snowy hill, over and over again, laughing into a gray, sparkling sky. The man beside him rolled over and over, too.

His mother hurled a snowball at Campbell, where he lay. It caught the coach in the heart like a fat bullet. She started to run. Campbell leaped up and ran after her, stooping to scoop snow, chasing her around a craggy-bark oak, catching her at last and rubbing snow across her cheeks and chin while she giggled and stumbled backward.

Kevin came after Campbell in mock revenge, carrying a snowball as big as a pumpkin.

Campbell backed off. "Hey! What're you going to do with that?" He pretended fear. "Hold everything!"

Kevin tossed it at him, and Campbell put his hands up, blocking it, shattering it.

He jumped at Kevin and grabbed him across the chest, under the arms, pulling him through the snow to some crusted low-hanging tree boughs. Before Kevin could squirm out of the way, Campbell had shaken the branches over his face, sending dollops of ice and slowly congealing fluff to smack against his forehead and hat.

He sat up, brushing at his eyes. His mother was on her back in a fresh patch of whiteness, arms and legs out wide, moving them back and forth to create an angel pattern, wings and gown. She was smiling, mouth open, tasting the delicious tumbling flakes.

Kevin took a gloved handful of snow and ate it.

Campbell began to bury Judy in drifts, tamping them firmly around and over her snowsuit, leaving only her happy eyes and grimacing lips, surrounded by glitter.

A snow day. No school. Kevin had awakened to the far-off bell of the telephone, followed by his mother's playful tossing of boots and mittens into his room. "Quick, before the roads get any worse," she had said. "We're going up to the museum." A few minutes after they had arrived, Campbell's red wagon lumbered into the parking lot, flinging snow from its back tires.

Campbell finished ice-packing Judy. "Now we'll dispose of you," the man teased, stalking Kevin.

Kevin—relishing the game—charged him suddenly,

pushing his shoulder into Campbell's jacket- and sweater-padded ribs and sending him to sprawl on his seat in a wet drift. Campbell snarled and got up on all fours. Kevin looked for refuge. He sprinted toward the "LOVE" statue, climbed high into the *L.* As Campbell lurched to his feet, Judy hit him from behind with a flying tackle and held on as he dragged her around and around.

From here Kevin could see a fragment of the river. Blue-white broomstick trees quivered on the opposite hills. He lay on his stomach, up across the *O,* and rested his head on his arms. Behind him, there was laughter and shouting, his mother's and Campbell's; beneath him, the statue's contours curved and dipped. The snow began to come faster, thick, sighing in downdrafts, collecting on his sleeves. Cottony. *His father.* Startled, Kevin raised his head. His father?

He called up the stock black-and-white vision of Ronald Greer.

Father? The photograph held a tint of color. The color slowly bled and deepened. The man began to move as the frame got larger. *His father, placing cotton balls for snowbanks around the model railroad.*

Kevin closed his eyes, stunned.

His father. Taking snapshot after snapshot of Kevin next to a squarish, lumpy snowman. His father swinging him over the banister onto the stairs and following him up to bed, his father kneeling on the wooden floor with his face in the sheets, we thank you, O Lord, for the gladness of this day and for the love in this house, grant us peace and keep us safe through this night and always, amen, his father's eyes blue like sky and bright like sun, his father's skin misted with the tiniest pebbles of water, dusted with minute golden hairs, shaded tan where he shaved, his father's kiss, his father kissing him, not the polite bridge-of-the-nose kiss of neighbors and uncles, but a kiss of gratitude, gratitude and unspeakable cherishing, full on the mouth.

CHAPTER 23

Thursday, November 23, 1972

JUDY WATCHED Leona slice dry bread into cubes for turkey stuffing; she did it slowly and with precision, cutting each small square the same size. The confident age-speckled fingers began to peel the onions, cropping off both ends with a sharp blade and then pulling at the copper skin, tearing it, making it creak.

Judy sat close to the counter on a kitchen chair, snapping green beans, which she held in a colander.

They were all talked out. Judy had heard about the new baby's face—which remarkably resembled Carol Lynn's—had heard about walking the floor night after night, trying to soothe Heather's colicky tummy, had heard about the miniature hot-water bottle which Leona had purchased and which seemed to help the child. Leona had heard about Kevin's football victory, the big snow and the acquisition of a Frederic Remington at the museum.

Judy knew better than to get in the way of Leona's Thanksgiving preparations. Holidays, religious or not, were sacred to Leona, and she delighted in creating feasts and honoring tradition. She found perpetual joy in the prelude to seasons: the choosing and ironing of appropriate table linens; the polishing of silver; the arranging of a centerpiece. A front door wreath told passersby what mood was being celebrated inside.

And Leona knew all the crafts of custom. Cross-stitch for Valentine hearts. Hand coloring for Ukrainian Easter eggs. Candlemaking to seal the leaves of autumn, the holly berries of Advent. To each grandchild she had taught the infinite pleasures of the calendar, patiently showing them how to cut cookie witches and Santas and shamrocks . . . helping them gather backyard bounty and bring it in to shine in bowls or to grow melty under a warm iron, between pieces of waxed paper. She loved the endless cycle, served it with dedication.

Leona ceased chopping the second onion and cocked her head. Listening? Judy looked around and then back to Leona, who had laid the knife at the edge of the wooden cutting board.

Her mother-in-law stepped away from the pile of onion pieces. The skin around her eyes was heavily indented, bluish. "Would you . . . do this for me?"

Judy stood up quickly, setting the colander in the sink. "Sure. You all right?"

Wrong question. Leona was *always* all right. Even when she wasn't.

"Yes, I'm fine. Just a little tired from helping Carol Lynn." She sank into the chair.

"I'll get you some water," Judy said, alarmed, reaching for a glass and filling it from the tap. "Here." She thrust it into her mother-in-law's hands, and Leona drank.

"Go ahead, go ahead." Leona gestured at the half-finished stuffing. "It doesn't matter."

Judy, knowing it useless to press Leona about her health, picked up the knife and began to work.

Tuesday, November 28, 1972

"I'VE GOT GOOD news," Tom Wellington said. He dug into his briefcase and pulled out a business-size envelope. Judy and Leona stared at it. Tom set the briefcase next to the coffee table and rose slightly to lean across it and hand the envelope to Judy.

"This is the letter from the post commander," he said. "The one from Washington will follow shortly, and you'll receive it on the day of the ceremony. It will be signed by the President."

Leona got up from the rocker and walked over to stand beside Judy as she unfolded the paper.

"Oh!" Leona said, and put her hand on Judy's shoulder. But Judy was not yet comprehending the printed words. She studied them, looking for the key phrase, trying to understand what was so important that Tom would hand-deliver this message. Surely it had something to do with Ron's well-being, his whereabouts.

In recognition of . . . patriotism and valorous service . . . Major . . . Lieutenant Colonel . . .

"Judy," Leona said in the voice of a mother prompting her young daughter to say thank you for a gift.

Judy glanced up at Tom. "Is this. . . ? What is this? A promotion in rank?"

He smiled and nodded. "Light colonel."

Judy crumpled the letter into a tight ball, which she held in her fist. "I don't want it."

Leona said nothing but withdrew her hand and moved abruptly away from Judy to sit in the rocker again.

Tom's smile had turned to an openmouthed gape. "I can appreciate how you feel, Judy," he said, "but Ron has earned this. He is a career officer after all."

"I don't want it." She looked at her mother-in-law, whose face had gone ashen. "I think it's an insult for them to bring us this when they've never—in five years—brought us any word from him. They couldn't possibly be doing anything for him, to get him in touch with us or to get him out. This is a joke." Judy glared at Tom and let the balled-up letter roll from her hand onto the carpet. "A joke."

"We're not meaning to attack *you*, Major Wellington," Leona offered graciously. "You've been very kind."

Tom addressed Judy. "I'm sure they have tried . . . to get him out, to get letters from him. Something. I believe that. If I didn't, I couldn't stay with them. I'm on your side. You know that. It's just an unfortunate set of circumstances."

"Unfortunate? It sure as hell is. And here's the bottom line: They don't like me. They never did. They play games with me."

Tom shook his head. "No."

"Judy," Leona said softly. "What would Ron want you to

do? Wouldn't this mean something to him? For all the time he's put in?"

Judy crossed her arms. "Tell the commander to tell the Pentagon or the President—or whoever—that if they want Ron to have the silver leaf cluster, they should find him and hand it to him. I'm not coming up there for any ceremony."

Tom closed his briefcase. "He's been promoted anyway, Judy. He's a lieutenant colonel. I'm sorry. That's the way it is, whether you want to accept the paper work or leave it in his file."

After Tom had left, Leona picked up the letter and sat silently in the rocker, smoothing the wrinkled paper out against her knees, touching the paragraphs, reading them over and over. "He'd be pleased by this," was all she said to Judy.

Wednesday, November 29, 1972

CAMPBELL WHEELED his car into Kevin's driveway. "Good practice, Kevin. You're a heck of a player. See you Friday."

"Okay, Coach. Thanks for the ride," Kevin answered.

"I'm glad it's the last game of the season," Justin muttered. "It's getting too darned cold."

Kevin got out of the car. "See ya." His stomach was growling. Almost suppertime. His mother would be here soon, and they could eat.

The door was unlocked; the warmth of the house flew against his face, making the skin burn. He headed straight for the kitchen.

Leona was lying on the linoleum floor, half under the kitchen table. She turned her head toward him as he came in and stretched her arm forward, pointing at him. Her features were shaped into a white, agonized mask.

His ears began to ring. She was getting ready to fall a

great distance, backward, away from him, through a terrible space. He ran over and clasped her hand, to hold her back, but she was already falling, had already begun to fall. Her hand was slippery; he couldn't keep her with him; there was already a tremendous downward momentum. He wouldn't be strong enough.

"Wait," he shouted. "I'll get help." He let go of her and ran for the kitchen door, out into the deserted driveway.

"Campbell! Come back!" he called, racing toward the street. "Joe! Joe Campbell!" The red wagon was far down the lane; he would never hear. *Oh, please,* he said to himself. He barreled into the middle of the street and dashed after the car. "Campbell!"

The red taillights came on. The car paused and started a slow reverse. Kevin waved his arms. The car came toward him, faster.

"What is it?" Campbell said, leaning out the window.

"My grandma, she's sick. Hurry!"

Campbell zipped past him and bounced the car into the driveway. Kevin heard the crunch of the emergency brake, and then Campbell was sprinting with him, to the kitchen door.

The coach stopped when he saw Leona; his eyes narrowed, assessing her. "Mrs. Greer?" He knelt down and took her pulse. "Mrs. Greer . . . can you talk to me? Can you tell me what's the matter?"

She bent her fingers and pressed the knuckles against the center of her chest.

Campbell gently pushed her hand aside and put an ear to her breastbone. He came up suddenly. "Kevin, call an ambulance."

"No," his grandmother pleaded.

"Do it," Campbell barked.

"No." She tried to sit up, but an invisible blow seemed to catch her midway. Campbell put an arm under her shoulders.

"What are you saying? You don't want to go to the hospital?" He stared at Kevin. "What does she mean?"

Kevin knew. The commotion of an ambulance would shame her. "She doesn't like to be sick."

"Well, she *is* sick. She might be having a heart attack. This is nothing to fool with."

Leona was looking older, second by second. Her skin, deeply lined, had come loose on her skull, as though this were the starting point for shedding her body. The struggle with Campbell was causing her to shrink rapidly away from her flesh and bones, her eyes and teeth. She would disappear altogether. But she would not consent. Not if it killed her.

Wind whistled in her throat. "I don't want that, an ambulance."

"You take her," Kevin said. "In the car." He glanced at Justin, who was hunched against a wall, looking frightened.

"Yes." Leona clutched feebly at Campbell.

"All right. I will. Hush now." Campbell smoothed the hair back out of her eyes with tenderness. "It's all right."

She grew quiet.

He put his cheek to Leona's forehead for a moment. "You're a tough customer, Mrs. Greer," he said, and lifted her into his arms.

The Intensive Care waiting room of Methodist Hospital was narrow—just a tad bigger than a walk-in closet—and smelled of ashes. Kevin could tell by looking at the ashtrays that they had been emptied countless times without being washed. The magazines were dog-eared and coffee-stained; the orange vinyl upholstery held brown scratches. Even the view from the lone window had been dismal: a misty panorama of brick buildings and warehouses. Now that it was dark, only a few faint lights winked out of the fog.

How long had he been in here? The overheads in the corridor had been turned out much earlier. He guessed it was at least ten-thirty, maybe more. His mother had been in and out of the waiting room all evening, busy with phone calls to relatives. Once every hour, for ten minutes, she had been permitted to visit Leona. Now she had gone somewhere with the doctor, who wanted to speak privately to her. Kevin resented the hospital's policy toward children. Because he was twelve, he had been allowed into the hospital, but then confined to this waiting room. He had not even glimpsed his grandmother since they took charge of her at the emergency entrance.

Campbell and Justin had left; Wellington had been there and gone. Kevin had refused dinner but now felt weak, and nauseated by the cigarette-cigar residue. This place was sad as hell, this waiting room. So many people had used it—miserable, anxious people whose lives had changed here, against their will. The marks and dents were proof of their numbers, but that didn't comfort him at all. Just made him feel more lonely . . . as though—if all those people had done it—it must surely be his turn.

He heard his mother's footsteps, her distinct gait, in the hallway. She came in, sighing.

"I don't think we can do any more tonight, but I'm afraid to leave."

"Why?"

"The doctor says that the first twelve hours are critical."

Kevin stared at her mouth, trying to read her meaning. "She's not going to die."

"It's possible."

"Tonight? She might die tonight?"

"They can't say for sure what's going to happen."

He had never considered this. Leona was permanent. Like the stars. He could find his way by staying close to her. She knew the answers to all the important questions; he merely needed to follow her.

"She can't die," he said.

"I feel that way, too."

"I want to see her."

"Kevin, they won't let you in the Intensive Care Unit."

"But what if she . . . goes . . . and I don't get to say good-bye?"

She nodded, sadly. "I know."

"I want to say something to her. She *can't* go until I get to talk to her. People don't just go like that and not say good-bye."

His mother's eyes filled with tears. "They do if they can't help it. I'll tell her. Whatever you want."

Kevin put the heels of his hands against his eyelids. "I'll make them let me in there."

She took his elbow and gently steered him to the couch; they sat on the edge of it. "If it comes to that, I'll speak for you, to get you in. I know how you feel."

"I should have called the ambulance."

"The doctor said it wouldn't have made any difference. You got her here very quickly. Don't blame yourself. It's a mistake to think that everything that happens has to be somebody's fault." She began to rub his back. "Should we go home and rest or should we stay?"

"Stay."

Thursday, November 30, 1972

KEVIN LAY ON his bed in the early-morning aura, feeling the sleep chemicals slowly engulf the back of his brain. He and Judy had left the hospital cafeteria at dawn. Leona's condition had not changed all night, and they had emerged from the building groggy, uncertain of their steps as if they themselves had been ill; the parking lot pavement jarred their bones.

Along the streets life had moved as usual: traffic, starting and stopping to the rhythm of signals; winter birds crouching on window ledges, their wings hunched up around their necks like coat collars; a few suited men carrying briefcases. *My grandmother is sick,* Kevin wanted to yell at them. *She might be dying. You should know it.*

Kevin shifted onto his side, reading the desk clock. Eight-thirty. School was in session. *Did you hear?* the kids would be saying. *Did you hear, did you hear . . .*

After a long, dreamless time Kevin awoke. His tongue was sticky, and he was sweating heavily. The room and the house beyond were infinitely quiet. A fragile layer of dust, like muffling snow, covered the dresser top. He studied its evenness, its fuzzy tranquillity.

Absence. Was that what he felt?

Was she gone?

He sat bolt upright on the tangled bedspread; there was a wall of water just beyond his bedroom. Soundless. Thick. Dividing him forever from his familiar world.

He ran toward it, hurtling himself through it, along the balconied hallway to his mother's room. The bed was made; sunlight spilled across its quilted daisies. His mother was dressed in a plum-colored suit and high-heeled shoes, putting on her earrings before the vanity mirror. She turned when she heard him. The gold earring she was winding into place flashed brilliantly, making him blink.

"Leona died," he said.

"No, honey. I just talked with the hospital. She's doing better." She hesitated, recognizing his disbelief. "She is, Kevin. They think she's going to be fine."

"Call again."

"They would call *us*, the minute that anything changed."

Then what did he feel that was so awful? He walked around the room slowly with his hands on his hips.

Things unsaid. That was what had bothered him most. Learning that someone he cared about could be yanked instantly from his life, leaving him with unspoken words like stones in his mouth.

He leaned against the doorjamb, looking at the telephone which did not ring, puzzling over the wall of water which was still tangible to him, which separated him now from his mother, made him so alone.

Silence. That's what it was, the water. His own silence. Mysterious. Unmoving.

Useless.

"I love you," he said aloud to her. She smiled and opened her arms to him.

CHAPTER 24

JUDY STOOD at the foot of the bed, waiting for Leona's pleased reaction as she awakened and focused on her son Bill.

Fear came into Leona's eyes. She scowled at him. Judy noticed that the soft beeps of her heart-monitoring equipment began to speed up.

"Hi, Mom," he said.

"Why are you here? Judy . . . Judy!" The voice was frail. Judy came around the bed to stand at Bill's elbow.

"Why is he here?"

Bill flushed with embarrassment. "I knew you were sick. I wanted to see you."

Leona eyed Judy and motioned for her to lean down, and Judy did. "Am I dying?" she whispered. "Tell me the truth."

"Of course you're not dying," Bill said kindly.

"You're not dying, Leona. We thought maybe you were, so I called Bill. You'll be all right."

She held Judy's gaze for a long moment. "Are the others here?"

"Yes, I called them."

She frowned.

I shouldn't have done it, Judy thought. *But what if I hadn't, and she had died?*

"Bill . . ." Judy straightened up and touched his shoulder, guiding him closer to his mother. "You go ahead and talk with her. They give us only ten minutes an hour."

Leona studied him. Seeing Ron, no doubt. He was so like Ron. But taller, with a few more pounds.

"I appreciate it, dear," she said to him, "but I'd really like to speak with Judy."

Bill patted her hand and stepped away, left the room.

Leona tilted her head and regarded the monitoring machines. "I know what's going to happen."

"You're not going to die," Judy assured her again. "Please believe me."

"I don't mean that. The children. They'll have to decide what to do with me. I don't want that, for someone to have to take care of me."

"But we'd all be happy to."

"I'll hate it. Somebody will get stuck with me. I won't be able to stand it."

Her children had discussed this privately when Nugget died and Leona began to live with each of them, four months at a time. If she should become ill, they had decided—too ill to travel comfortably—she would stay wherever she was. Indefinitely. A game of musical chairs: When the music stopped, Leona stayed.

Judy would be the caretaker.

"You kids can't fool me," Leona said. "You already had it worked out, didn't you? You're the one who has to do it, isn't that right?"

"It's not that I have to. I want to. I want you with me." Judy spoke to the loneliness in Leona's eyes.

"What about the museum?"

"I'll take a leave."

"I don't want any fighting in the family on account of this—who has to take care of me."

Her husband's mother. The mother of her husband. *Oh, Ron.* She kissed Leona's forehead with pity and affection. "I'll fight to keep you."

Saturday, December 2, 1972

JUDY INHALED the aroma of roast turkey and cornbread stuffing, of rich gravy and black coffee. Her soul ate of the free laughter, the spirited voices. Chairs shook. There were childhood stories and loud teasing. Judy devoured them all, filling herself. She couldn't get over the wonder of looking from one face to the next, down her long dining table, glimpsing Ron in many guises. Here were assembled his brothers and sisters, and his only child. She had needed this, through the bleak years of his absence, but had not recognized it. Illness and funerals, that was the way of it for families: the only occasions when money was spent for impromptu travel, the effort put forth to take time from work. Had she realized how much she needed to see them all together like this, had she told them, they would have come at once. But it had never happened. Now, for Leona's illness, they had converged.

Dear ones! She scanned their faces, finding Ron's face in theirs, feature by feature. Bill had Ron's hair and skeletal structure. Sharon, his blue eyes. Judy could see her husband's nose in the shape of Carol Lynn's. Gretchen had his speech pattern, the forthright, witty style, the muted accents of a dozen Army-assignment cities. And Ed . . . had Ron's teeth. She found this one the strangest of all. To look at Ed's smile was to stare directly at her husband's handsome jaw. Their teeth were the same size, the same shade and even arched in the same flawless formation. Flawless except for one tooth on the bottom left, near the front, which sat sideways in its slot. Just like Ron's. Exactly.

And Kevin. So similar to his father, getting to resemble him more and more. Kevin seemed overwhelmed—overjoyed—by this gathering, the hugging and the fun, the reminiscing. No one in the Greer family merely told a story; they acted it out with wild animation, with altered voices and large gestures, with standing up and sitting down.

"Dad's really sore," Ed was saying, winding into another tale and starting to laugh. "He takes off after Bill, up the stairs. Remember?"

The others nodded, grinning.

Ed took a gulp of his coffee. "Bill runs up and locks himself in with Ron—in Ron's room. Ron hears the door rattling and Dad bellowing, and he figures in another minute the old guy's gonna knock the door down. So Ron gets out his Boy Scout rope and ties it around Bill, under his shoulders, and lowers him out the window. Meanwhile, Dad gives up and goes downstairs to wait. But when he gets down there, he walks past a window and sees Bill's feet swingin'. Dad lets out a holler that can be heard from here to Christmas. He thinks Bill's hung himself over the whole thing!"

Carol Lynn laughed gaily. "You characters!"

Bill took up the story. "He flies back upstairs. Starts banging on the door like mad. Ron jumps a mile and lets go of the rope. I must have dropped seven or eight feet. That didn't tickle! But I got up and took off, I can tell you."

"And left Ron to face the music," Sharon said.

Bill chuckled. "Hey, by that time Dad's whole life had passed in front of him; he figured, *Lord, if you save this kid, I'll never get after any of 'em again.* So when Ron opens the door to square off with Dad, the ol' man he just runs to the window and he sees I'm okay; then he turns to Ron and grabs him in this colossal hug, yelling like a bayonet fighter. *Hah, huh, huh, ya, huh!* Glad as hell, he was."

"God!" Gretchen laughed.

"And he never chased any of us again," Carol Lynn said, holding up one finger.

"I wouldn't have opened the door," Kevin said.

"Oh, shoot, Ron was like that," Bill answered. "He'd take up for any of us. He never seemed to care who could whip him and who couldn't. He'd just get in there. In between."

That was Ron. Judy had heard this legend before and believed it to the letter.

Carol Lynn glanced at Judy. "Maybe we shouldn't . . . Does this make you sad?"

"No!" She didn't have to say more. They were right with her. It made him alive again, the telling of his antics. "Do you"—it was safe; she could trust them—"think he's still there? I mean, do you feel it? Inside?"

They looked from one to the other.

"I do," Kevin said quickly. His tone held amazement. For her doubt? For her honesty? To lose faith was to be guilty if Ron became lost for good. Their faith was the only thing that held him there in time and space.

"I don't think he's"—Bill ran his fingers through his yellow hair—"dead. I don't feel that at all." He gazed questioningly at his brothers and sisters.

"He isn't," Gretchen stated flatly. "If he were, I'd know it."

Carol Lynn nodded. So did Ed.

"Sharon?" Judy asked.

Sharon, the quiet, fragile one, peered into the candle flame, concentrating. "He isn't," she said. "He's not."

Not dead! If he were, one of them would feel it.

He was among them. In the joyous remembering, they had somehow called forth the essence of him. Everything but the precious living body.

If our combined will can do this, Judy thought, *we can bring him back. We can pick him out of wherever he is, no matter how far. We can deliver him.*

Saturday, December 9, 1972

JOE CAMPBELL opened the draperies in Leona's bedroom, and morning sun poured in. Leona, dwarfed by the four-poster bed and a hill of covers, scarcely moved.

"I brought you these," he said, holding up a bouquet so that Leona could see it: white mums and pink carnations, baby's breath, a pale yellow ribbon.

"Beautiful! Here, I'll put them in water." Judy came forward and took them, paused in the doorway.

"I've been worried about you," Joe said to Leona. "I'm glad you're home."

She stirred. "Thank you for the flowers."

"Do you mind if I stay a minute?" Joe asked.

"You can stay a lot of minutes," Leona answered. "I

might be here forever." She still had some punch to her: a good sign. Judy noted that Leona's voice had become stronger during the past week.

Joe sat in the wide brown recliner which he had moved, with Kevin's help, up the steps into Leona's room.

"This is going to be boring," Leona said glumly. She looked exhausted from the ambulance ride home. Well, perhaps that was more mental than physical.

"I don't see how a visit from me could possibly be boring," Joe kidded her.

"Boring to lie in bed," Leona replied. "How long do I have to do this?"

"Knowing you, not very long," Judy told her.

But Leona was melancholy. She stared at the ceiling with obvious resentment. Her body had failed her. The central thing she had counted on in her disciplined no-madic life had disappointed her.

Judy exchanged a distressed glance with Campbell.

"Since the first day home is bound to be the toughest," he announced to Leona, "I've arranged for a concert."

She turned her head in his direction.

"Don't thank me," he protested, raising his hands. "It was the least I could do."

Leona pursed her lips in mild amusement.

"You happen to see before you," he said grandly, "a champion whistler, winner of Hartford's High-and-Mighty Contest: Joseph Campbell, called out of retire-ment for this command performance. Put your feet up and enjoy a musical medley by one of the world's greatest showmen!"

That got a smile from Leona.

Joe leaned back in the recliner until the footrest popped out. He took a deep breath and began to whistle the first strains of "The High and the Mighty." Judy expected it to be a joke, off-key and without sufficient wind.

He started slowly, softly, the tune clear and rich. The notes slid into one another, full-textured and astonish-ingly pleasant. They gathered volume but retained a delicate, almost Oriental air. Joe directed the music at Leona, as if he were serenading her; by and by the two relaxed away from each other, and the melody seemed to float along the walls, to surround them. He whistled a second song, and then a third. "High Noon," "My Heart's in the Highlands."

"That's my 'High' medley." He laughed. And began again.

Leona seemed to glide across the music to a place of contentment. She rolled slightly onto her left hip and studied the man, who was whistling now toward the farthest corner of the room and beyond that to a cloud in the open sky.

"You can't sleep?" Judy bent over Leona, examining her face in the dim glow of the night-light.

"No."

"It's nearly midnight. Shouldn't you try? Can I get you anything?"

"No. Thank you."

Leona seemed groggy enough. Her eyelids drooped, her speech was slow.

"Well . . ." Judy sat in the recliner, wrapping her flannel gown around her legs. "I don't like to just . . . leave you like this."

"I can call you."

"I put the brass bell—the one Nugget brought back from Austria—right here on the bedstand. Ring that if you need me."

"All right." There was an undertow to Leona's despondency.

"Can't you say what it is?" Judy coaxed. "Is it . . . being sick?"

Leona sighed. "When I start to fall asleep, sometimes I don't breathe. Or I think I don't breathe. It's not automatic anymore, the breathing. I wake myself up with it and try to remember how to do it. I can barely get going."

Terrifying. It was not like Leona to admit weakness, tell

any part of herself. It must be so: that she couldn't breathe as she did before. Certainly it was possible that whatever regulated her breathing closed down at intervals during her sleep.

"Did this happen in the hospital, too?"

"Yes. But they were always there, to make sure. I knew they wouldn't let me go."

"The nurses?"

"Um." Leona swallowed.

Judy stood up and got a blanket from the cedar chest, drew it around herself and stretched out in the recliner. "You rest now. I'll watch, and make sure. I'll be here."

Leona's gradual journey away from Judy's eyes wound through years of trees. At first the branches were bare, but dead leaves soared up from the ground and covered them plentifully, like feathers. The leaves became supple, blushed scarlet and amber, dark green and then foam green, pale. Transparent. They folded unto themselves, curling into tight coral buds, squeezing, smaller ... smaller, flattening against their branches. Disappearing.

She grew cold. A fresh batch of brown leaves arose in a rush from the thawing soil to stick to the trees, and a new warmth touched her.

"Come and live with us," she had said to Nugget's mother, "go where we go." And Nugget's mother, pleased, did.

Scarlet, amber, green, foam pale, curling ...

Here is the old lady now, Leona thought, walking past her. The poor soul could not hold her head up and was tied into her chair, about the waist, like a drooling baby.

"Come live with us, come live with us," her mother-in-law cried out, to no one in particular. She had done that, Leona recalled: had sung out that same sentence over and over during her final months, as though it were the only thing she could remember of her ninety-three years. Whole collections of words had vanished. But that one phrase, That One, was a coin, a rosary she used ... the most beloved thing she could still find . . . to grip as she made her passage.

Coral buds, flat bark.

It was cold again; but the leaves danced upward, and the scattered silver evening drew together into a round autumn sun-ball. Warmth arrived, shimmering.

There were only a few shadows left clinging to the eyelet bedcover. She had slept the night.

Leona's blurry vision settled on Judy; her sweet, determined face came into focus, the eyes red-rimmed but still ardently watchful.

CHAPTER 25

Saturday, December 16, 1972

"MY GOD, Judy, you look awful." Susan set a big cardboard box down on the foyer tile. A fat terrier was curled up inside, panting, lying listlessly on a nest of towels.

"Who's this?"

"Antoinette. She's very pregnant. I couldn't leave her at home. You look awful."

"I heard you the first time."

"Has it been that bad? I mean . . ." Susan raised her eyes toward Leona's room.

Judy put a finger to her lips and motioned Susan into the living room.

"What?" Susan asked, shedding her coat. "Why didn't you call me sooner?"

"I thought I could handle it. But I need a rest. She's much better. Really, she is."

"Did you tell her I was coming?"

"Yes. It's fine with her. She knows I need a break. I told her I was going over to sack out at your house."

"You've been up with her at night? You look like you never sleep."

"She's afraid at night . . . that she'll stop breathing. Do you think you could sit next to her tonight and watch her?"

"Sure. Go on—get your stuff and get out of here. Don't come back till morning."

"Here's a number where I can be reached." Judy thrust it into Susan's hand. "Put it away. In your purse."

Susan read the paper, then folded it carefully.

"And could you try to keep her from hearing the news? Maybe . . . talk to her instead of putting on the TV."

"What news?"

"Where have you been all day?"
"Washing my dogs and taking naps."
"The peace talks fell through again."
"Shit."

Judy drove sleepily along the narrow two-lane road toward Joe Campbell's house. Her headlights followed the yellow median through a moonless night; the rearview mirror reflected only blackness. Following the median was like following string back out of a thick, confusing forest. When she came to the end of it, she would be in the clearing, safe. With Joe.

She pulled onto his dirt road. He was expecting her. He would smile and hug her; he would make herb tea and poached eggs for a late supper. They would lie by the fire, drinking wine, until she fell asleep in his arms.

She parked the car in the driveway, behind his, and ran up onto the porch.

"Joe!" She knocked at the screen door. Lights were blazing inside, but she could not see him moving about. "Joe." She knocked again. The front porch lamp had not been lit, and the foreign night crawled right up to her boots.

She tried the knob. Locked.

Judy glanced uneasily around, out across the bushes. Then she left the porch and went to the living room window, stood on tiptoe. Too high. She couldn't see in. She began to feel an anger beating about in her chest. He had known she was coming! Was he in the shower or what?

She strode purposefully toward the birdhouse; she had to go past the window glow into deep shadow. Now she could see clearly: a chair, the fireplace, the back of the couch. A man's stockinged foot, on the floor . . . visible just beyond the end of the couch.

What if?

She darted to the window and pounded on it. No answer. Horror flooded into her. She clung to the porch railing for support, skimming her gaze along a tree line that led to the back of the house.

I'm afraid they'll hurt you, Joe.

"Is someone out there?" she shouted into the enormous silence. "Come and get me. Come on! I want to see you."

She waited, sweating, adrenaline pumping through her limbs. She was ready.

No one came forward.

"Cowards!" she screamed.

She knew how to get in the damned house. Joe had told her. Through the cellar. *Joseph.* She stumbled through the darkness, toward the side of the house, falling, picking herself up, using her hands to find the slanted cellar doors. One was already open. She pulled on the other, and it came up, groaning. She laid it back and sat on the cold cement, slid down the steps into the fearsome hole.

"Joe!" Judy haltingly made her way across the abyss, picturing where the stairs must be, groping for them.

Was someone behind her?

Here. The stairs. She scrambled up, up, and twisted the doorknob. The powerful light of the kitchen hit her like a blow, making her wince. "Joe!"

And then she was in the living room, bending over his body which was spread out on the carpet, eyes closed. What was wrong? She scanned him: Army-green socks . . . blue jeans . . . plaid flannel shirt . . . stereo earphones.

"Please!" She touched his chin.

He woke up—startled—and rolled to a sitting position, tearing off the headset. "Judy?"

She threw herself against his chest, whimpering.

"Hey." He stroked her hair. "Let me . . ." He laid the headset up on the couch and embraced her with strong arms. "What's the matter, sweetheart?"

"Why didn't you answer me?"

"Well, I didn't . . . I must have fallen asleep with the earphones on. I was listening to music. I'm sorry. You came in through the basement?"

She nodded, trying to control her shivering.

"Oh." He cradled her, rocking her, pulling her face close to his until she was breathing the sweet, comforting scent of his neck. "I'm so sorry. You thought something happened to me, didn't you?"

"That they had come to get you," she said. "I thought I felt them out there."

"No, no. Never. Nobody's trying to hurt us. You feel mad at them, the Army, the government. That's why you're afraid." He kissed her eyelids. "If anything, they would want to help you. That's what they'd try to do."

"They're going to start it all over again. The war. The killing. The bombs."

"They won't." He held her tighter. "Believe me."

Wednesday
December 20, 1972

Dearest Judy,

Merry (?) Christmas. I think of you each day and hope that Leona is getting better and better. It is so typically unselfish of you to take a leave from your job to nurse her.

I know this is a Christmas card, and I'm supposed to say jolly things, so let me think. Hum.

I truly hope that the coming year will see the end of all your waiting and the beginning of the good life. You certainly deserve it, dear friend. May 1973 be the year that Ron comes home. Grant and I send you and your family all our love.

Here comes Part II. If you don't want to keep this end of the letter, you can cut it off and throw it away. But I don't lie to you, do I? I am sizzling—even puking (literally)—over the renewed bombing. It's insane! Hideous & disgusting. This is the third day in a row that King Nixon's tried to blow Hanoi and everything else in North Vietnam completely off the map.

We have to make them stop! I beg you to help us. Please. Come back into the movement. The country watches you. Get in front of the cameras again. We're going to have a giant protest at the inauguration. The biggest. Be there? (I'm on my knees, Judy.)

Grant's a wreck. This bombing, it's twice as vicious. Murder. He has much guilt. It's a circus here. The girls don't know what to make of him. I can't wait for Christmas so they can get their dolls and whatnot. Distract them. He stays glued to that stuff on TV. A magnet. Furious. They get in his way and there's trouble.

How have you kept your sanity? I'm not kidding. I really want to know. You seem like you've come to terms all of a sudden. I admire. I'm still trying to find the handle. The Air Force should send us a live-in counselor. They owe us!

Okay, okay, I'll wrap it up. But of all my Christmases, this one is the most bitter. I think of you worrying about Ron stuck in the B-52 fireworks. I worry, too.

Time to chop off this half of the letter and throw it in the john. Merry Christmas anyway.

Here are some kisses for Kevin and Leona. Keep several for yourself.

Connie

Sunday, December 24, 1972

IT HAD BEEN hours since Judy and Kevin had trimmed the Christmas tree. He had gone off to the church candlelight service, leaving Judy and Leona to sip tea next to the fragrant boughs.

The seventh day of the bombing. Judy could hear the mantel clock ticking away the tragic minutes.

The two women sat close together on the sofa in the glitter of tiny, winking lights. Each strand was all white, a string of pearls. Judy and Kevin had bought the biggest tree they could carry and had had to saw quite a bit off the trunk to make it fit their living room.

Leona set her cup down with a click.

They both stared at the tree as if it could talk. The ornaments were their heritage. Treasured jewels. The symbols of significant personal events. Leona had brought her own: perhaps five dozen keepsakes that chronicled her years, like charms on a bracelet. They were Indian and African, Russian, Mexican. There was a glossy Swiss sled from her girlhood and a teak cross from her wedding.

Judy's ornaments were windows to the past, with Ron behind each one: a golden rocker from the year Kevin was born; an olive shell from their Florida honeymoon; an ark of animals for the year a flash flood had caught them on a summer hike and they had climbed through branches onto a hillside.

Their marriage was a book she had read and liked: distant. Unreal. But he? She could still feel his flesh, stand face-to-face with him. He was vivid, an actual presence: the blond, rumpled hair and kind eyes; the energetic tilt of the head and surprising sinew of the neck. There was always a tinge high on his cheekbones as though he had just come in from a stinging storm. He was earnest in his speech, precise; the tenor of it was low and resonant, sturdy, large. It inspired peacefulness. He could lull his son to sleep in the length of a prayer.

She studied all the little windows of the Christmas tree, seeing a green day here, an overcast day of strawberry picking there. With him. A man of infinite gentleness. A man who would throw live shells back into the sea, a man who would make a U-turn on a crowded highway to pluck up an injured dog.

Is that why she had waited for him? Because she knew a betrayal would crush his heart?

There was more. Her heady desire for him; her pleasure in his strong, lean body. She remembered it totally: his passion for her, his ceaseless fascination with her from the first time that they hesitatingly kissed at the end of the Sunday bus ride. In broad daylight.

His tenderness, his sensuality . . . who could say which was the most of it? Husband. That's what he was.

Always.

And she had learned the thoughts of widows, the constant mirage: glimpsing a reflection of the beloved in a shopwindow and whirling to find only a stranger with his peculiar gait or his length and hue of hair or a jacket like the one she had given him the Christmas before he went away.

"I'm going. January first," Leona said.

"Where?"

"To Sharon's. That's the day I'm supposed to."

Leona might be well enough to travel but . . . No! Judy didn't want that—for her to pack and disappear. Leona gave the house a coziness, a feeling of direction; they were passengers in a railcar, a rosy illumination moving steadily through midnight countryside. They were coming from; they were going to. Not lost, simply in transit. Leona could see the track.

"Stay with me." Judy reached over to take her mother-in-law's hand. "I need you."

"You've done enough for me." Leona bowed her head and was quiet for many seconds. "But I will . . . I would like to . . . stay. Just a bit longer." She lifted Judy's fingers and pressed them to her cheek.

Sunday, December 31, 1972

JUDY CROSSED the street in front of her house and stepped over the sooty snowdrift which lined the curb. Joe would be waiting at the corner. She hurried along the ice-slick sidewalk, in and out of the streetlamp circles.

He was there, at the vacant lot. They kissed silently, eagerly, and strolled toward the field and the meadow. They could barely see each other in the receding glimmer of porch bulbs.

"I can't stay long. Kevin will worry. He's watching Leona while I take a walk. She's asleep."

"Is her breathing better?" Joe asked.

"Yes. We don't have to sit up with her at night."

He ran his fingertips along her jawline. "It's so good to see you, Judy. I really missed you."

"I missed you, too. How was Christmas in Connecticut?"

"Snowy, same as here."

"Happy New Year." She impulsively slid her arms around his neck, and they kissed again. A slow, joyful kiss; a kiss of excitement, of devotion.

This man felt like a husband to her. Blessedly familiar. The thought made a chill inch along the nape of her neck. She had never contemplated choosing between Ron and Joe. She had not meant for it to come to that.

Stunned, she pressed her face against the lapel of his overcoat.

"Tell me."

"The bombing," she said, tucking her hands under his arms for warmth. "Fourteen days now."

"There's a cease-fire."

"Just for New Year's. You know that."

"I doubt the raids will go on much longer."

"I need to do something, Joe. To speak out. And I will. Leona's nearly strong enough. I can't shake her up right now, though."

"When?"

"In a couple of weeks. At the inauguration."

"Will Kevin be strong enough for you to shake *him* up?"

"I can't think about that. I have to fight the evil. It's winning." She could hear her words cracking, becoming strident.

"Have you been getting some rest?"

"More and more. She's well enough that I can go back to work Tuesday." Weariness, a companion. Judy no longer wore it gracefully but carried it heavily about. December had been a kaleidoscope of endless stair climbing, changing and laundering of sheets, meal preparation, dishwashing and difficult physical assistance—helping Leona from bed to chair to bathroom to table. Reading to her. Combing her hair. Banishing bad dreams.

"Is she going to be able to get along by herself?" Joe asked.

"Yes. She's looking forward to it. Leona's tough. A soldier. That's how she lives. I doubt that anything could really break her spirit."

Kevin walked noiselessly along the hallway and paused at the entrance to Leona's room. She was not in her bed.

Anxiety shot through him. Where was she? She had been sleeping only minutes ago. He was responsible for her; he had promised his mom.

He stepped farther into the room, his gaze sweeping the shadowy pillow, the thrown-back covers. She was sitting in the wooden chair by the window, with her back to him. He could see the frail arch of her spine in silhouette. She was leaning forward, peering into the street.

He came closer and opened his mouth to speak but closed it quickly when he noticed her expression. The streetlamp just beyond the pane cast exaggerated peaks and hollows into her face. In the familiar landscape of his grandmother's smiles and frowns he had not ever seen this curious slant to her eyes, this quizzical parting of the lips. It was a look that small children have when listening to grown-ups, trying to understand their crowded sentences.

She was clearly staring at something.

He sensed a danger in letting her know he was there. Two cautious steps behind her brought him to a full view of the sidewalk opposite their house. His mother and Joe Campbell were down the street a ways, in a streak of dusty yellow light, shoving one another playfully, laughing. He couldn't hear their laughter, but he could tell it was soft, soft, like the sharing of a secret.

CHAPTER 26

What did it mean? Kevin hesitated only a moment, then turned and walked, deliberately flat-footed and silent, along the carpeted path to his room. *What were they doing?*

He couldn't understand. Maybe it was his point of view . . . like when he was little and had to get the paint-spattered three-step ladder to see how many cookies were left in the bottom of the jar. That was it: like being too short to see over the counter at the post office and then being lifted high in his father's arms suddenly to glimpse the scales and stamps, gray canvas bins and wooden sorting cubicles crammed with letters.

If I were Leona, I would see . . . What? He rubbed at the pulse which was racing in his cheeks. Through Leona's eyes, it would be wrong for his mother to be with a man other than his father. But Joe Campbell wouldn't try to . . .

Kevin inclined his head toward his grandmother's room, studying the faint outlines of picture frames and railing slats along the hallway.

A man and a woman. His mother. Joe Campbell.

She mustn't.

He snatched his jacket from its hook and pulled it on as he hurried toward the stairs. A fierce anger began to propel him, an outraged defense of his defenseless father.

He would not let it happen. He would stop her.

He could imagine Campbell's surprise as Kevin got between them, taking his mother by the arm to bring her home. Campbell would try to talk him out of his suspicions. But he knew better now.

Kevin took the last two stairs in one stride. The front door opened, and Judy came into the foyer, flicking on the overhead light. Her hair was mussed up, and she was smiling, drawing the lavender scarf from around her neck, wiping her feet on the braided rag rug.

She froze when she saw him. He noticed how the dabs of snow on the shoulders of her coat gleamed as they melted.

"What is it?" she asked. "Leona?"

Kevin shook his head. "Why were you out there with Campbell?"

She pressed the scarf to her stomach, and he could see fear come into her eyes.

"Mother?"

She watched his lips as he said, "You're thinking of loving him, aren't you?" She reminded him of a deer he had caught once with a flashlight; she stood perfectly still, amazed and frightened. Then something made her look behind him. And up. The color left her face.

Oh, my Lord, no. Sweet Jesus, no, she prayed, staring at her mother-in-law, who was sitting on the top step in her nightgown.

The end of everything. Her marriage. Her family. Broken. Lost forever.

Leona gripped the banister and pulled herself up, to speak.

Judy couldn't move. Her bones were welded together, blazing inside her flesh.

"Kevin," Leona said. Her eyes met Judy's. With compassion. "You're making your mother feel terrible—making her think you don't trust her. That's not fair. Joe Campbell has offered us his friendship. We can have a lot of friends over a lifetime, both men and women. It doesn't mean we're giving up the other people we love. Don't be jealous."

Kevin examined his shoes in embarrassment and then whispered, "I'm sorry."

His sadness wrenched her heart. She deserved his fury. She was guilty.

"Kevin, I—"

"Judy," Leona interrupted, "would you please bring me a cup of tea? I'm having trouble sleeping."

"But—"

Be quiet, Leona's expression said. *I understand it all. Everything. Don't throw your life away. Be still.*

Judy sat on the edge of the bathtub, wiping her mouth with a cold washcloth. Another wave of nausea rippled through her. She concentrated on a decorative spray of leaves etched at the top of the medicine cabinet mirror. *What do I want?* she thought. *What do I really want?*

After nearly six years of waiting, after hundreds of letters written without answer, after being arrested and kicked and hated for her political activism, did she still want Ron? Was he still the goal? Or had her fighting and suffering led to an ironic conclusion: leaving him for a person she had known three months?

A light-headedness came. Judy clutched the sink for balance and put her cheek down on her hand. Three months with Joe Campbell, fourteen years with Ronald Greer. If she read that in a story, she would call the shorter relationship an affair. But that word was too slick, too uncharitable for what had happened to her. The man had changed her life, utterly. For the better. Changed the family, all three. Cared for them. Saved them. And each one knew it.

But . . . losing Ron. That would be unbearable. If she were too agonized right now to decide what might bring contentment in the long run, she could at least identify the worst of all nightmares: never to see, never to live with her husband again.

She and he were the two halves of a single being.

January 3, 1973
Wednesday

Dear Connie,
   Happy (?) New Year. You were right about the air raids. A token truce for each holiday, and they're back at it. I have changed my mind about a lot of things and am impatient with my own silence. Ashamed. Please put me in the front line at the inaugural protest. Will I have a chance to

speak out for Ron? I hope so. Just let me know how you're arranging it.
  I'll be taking a night flight from Indy on Friday the 19th. Count on me.

                              Love to you four,
                              Judeeeeeee

Tuesday, January 9, 1973

JOE STOPPED eating and decisively set his fork on his plate. "You're scaring me," he teased. "I feel like the condemned man having his last meal. First you want to meet me on neutral turf, and then you ignore an expensive dinner. What are we doing here?" He squinted at her. "Judy?"

She was seeing him at the coffee urn, scalding his hand and laughing at himself; she was seeing him on the football field, hugging her son. She loved Joe Campbell for so many reasons. In so many ways. The situation was complex beyond her imagining. She had never had patience with the concept that a woman could love two men at the same time. Such people were selfish, crude. If you had any goodness in your spirit, any morals at all, it was out of the question.

How, then, could it have happened?

"Hey." He frowned.

"Are you finished, ma'am?" The waiter regarded her barely touched plate of prime rib, baked potato and broccoli.

"Yes, I am."

He removed it. "Was there anything wrong with your dinner?"

"No. I'm not . . . hungry."

"Sir? Are you through?"

"Not yet," Joe said.

The waiter walked over and handed the plate to a busboy.

"I might as well try to eat it." Joe cut into his steak but

put his utensils down without taking a bite. "We're going to my house," he said firmly. "Together. Right now. I can't talk to you like this." Joe waved at the waiter, for the check.

If she went with him, she would not be able to say what she had come to say. He would surround her with his sensuality, his mystique.

"Joe . . ." Tears began to blur her vision. She blinked, and they spilled down her cheeks, dropping from her chin onto the front of her dress. "I can't come with you. I have to—I want to—stay with Ron."

Each word seemed like a boulder she was hurling at him, so much misery was reflected in his eyes.

He loved her. For some unfathomable reason he could not say it to her, could not even weep with her. If he could—if he suddenly stood up, pulling her from her chair and forcing her to go with him, she would not be able to say no.

He lowered his chin, spent a long moment digging in his pockets for his wallet and for a clean handkerchief, which he gave to her.

"I never . . . expected . . . anything else," he said.

In the parking lot they paused beside her car. How could she say good-bye to him? Where would she find the strength for it? He was looking at her in stunned silence.

He had given so much. What had she given him in return? What, really? How cruel she had been to use him. Why had she ever begun?

The tears came again. "I didn't mean to hurt you. You've been so good to me. I'm sorry, Joe." She closed her eyes, sobbing.

She felt him move nearer; his arms were around her, holding her. "Judy . . . don't," he whispered. "Don't, don't . . ."

"I can't stand it." She pulled away from him, wiping her cheeks with her hands.

Forgetting him was not possible, would never be possible. They would grow old and die—apart—but still loving in some way; she knew that. They would always wonder.

Had he remarried? Did she often think of him? Identical images of ecstasy and regret were imprinted on their brains ... pictures of each other, of this strange time.

He kissed his fingertips and touched them briefly to her trembling mouth. A determination came into his eyes. To keep her? To let her go?

She stepped away from him, as a sign.

He nodded and walked to his car without looking back.

Tuesday, January 16, 1973

LEONA SMELLED peace. She paused on the porch, drinking the aroma of it with pleasure before she started gingerly down the puddled lane. A January thaw was just what she needed. She wouldn't have her son coming home to an old lady! She had been strengthening herself bit by bit with indoor exercise, and today she would take some air.

They had stopped the bombing. Thank God for that. But bombing or no bombing, she had her own weather-vane, and she knew what she knew. She had caught the whiff of it before—Korea, World War II. It was as distinctive as the fragrance of springtime in a hard April rain.

Perhaps she had been infused with such perception by years as a military wife; she had the reverse ability to detect danger when it was not yet visible. She had urged them out of Hungary in time, hadn't she?

She believed strongly in things unseen and in a powerful ordering of the world. There was God, of course, first of all; and the intricate structure of His Creation. She gloried in the detail of His plan. She had faith that all items were numbered and sorted, awaiting their season.

Her years had been good. They had rested on the doctrine that events were being taken care of by beneficent forces; she had merely to live according to the rules. She put her trust in God and then in the government of the Greatest Country on Earth, and in its honorable Army, which had always so capably held her life and the lives of her loved ones in safekeeping.

These never failed.

Thursday, January 18, 1973

JUDY LAID aside some acquisition papers she had been signing and pushed the flashing button on her desk phone.

"Judy Greer."

"Judy, it's Susan." She was whispering.

"Susan?"

"Campbell's been reassigned."

Judy dropped the ball-point pen onto the blotter and swiveled her chair toward the telephone.

"He's been recalled to the Pentagon. February twelfth. His papers just came through."

Friday, January 19, 1973

JUDY MOVED her luggage forward again, toward the airline counter. She had been ninth in line, and now a lot of people were waiting behind her. She had figured it would be like this: crowded and possibly overbooked. So many people would be going from Indianapolis to Washington for the inauguration. Indy's Republican mayor was a good friend to Richard Nixon, and the President had treated this city accordingly. She imagined that lots of official invitations had been issued to the dignitaries of Marion County.

The man in front of her stepped away, and it was her turn. She hefted her suitcase onto the steel scale. "Judy

Greer," she said. "You're holding a ticket for me. Flight six-one-one to Washington."

The agent, a tall graying man with wire-rimmed glasses, thumbed through a stack of tickets. "Greer?"

"G-r-e-e-r."

He tapped the pile into an even-edged stack again and pressed some buttons on his console. "Flight six-one-one?"

"Yes." She could imagine all the impatient faces behind her.

"You're not listed for this flight, Mrs. Greer. Did you call in this reservation?"

"Yes, I did. Three weeks ago."

"I don't have a record of it." He was very apologetic. "Your name is not here, and this flight is full."

"How can that be? I reconfirmed it, the day before yesterday."

"I don't know. I'm very sorry. Would you like to stand by for a seat?"

Damned computer foul-up.

Or . . . had someone canceled it?

She slowly scanned the terminal to see if anyone was watching her. In the crush of bags and babies and coats and hurrying feet, she could find nothing sinister, no pair of eyes covertly observing her reaction.

"Would you care to stand by?"

The government.

Son of a bitch! She should have known! She should have picked up the ticket in advance. "I want to speak to your supervisor."

"I'll be glad to call him for you. Would you mind stepping to one side, please, so that we can serve the other passengers?"

The agent removed her suitcase from the scale and set it behind the counter. But Judy realized she would not be going anywhere. Not this time. Even if she had handed him a paid-for ticket, her name would have been absent from his list. A cancellation. A refund already in the mail.

Tonight would be spent wearing herself out, berating

the hapless supervisor, trying for seats on other airlines and standing by for this flight. None of it would matter.

They had her sewed up.

Monday, January 22, 1973

SHE WAS WAITING for Tom, perched on a fender of his car, when he left work. He brightened when he saw her.

"Hi, Judy! Welcome! How are you?"

"Very funny."

"What's wrong?"

"I presume the information goes both ways in this chain of command. I want you to relay a message."

He raised an eyebrow. "I hope it's not bad news. They kill the messenger when he brings bad news. Come on, let's sit in the car and put on the heater." He unlocked it.

"No, thanks. A hundred thousand protesters showed up at the inauguration on Saturday, and I wasn't one of them. I was right here. I spent the entire weekend at home, watching it on TV, courtesy of the Pentagon. But they're not going to keep me quiet. No way. I'll be smarter next time. You tell them that."

"You didn't go?" He seemed surprised.

"My airline reservation mysteriously disappeared."

A flush inched across his forehead. "And you think the Army did that?" She could sense his resentment.

"Tell them," she said, slipping off the fender and starting away.

He grabbed her arm. "Hold it. This is all out of shape. Can't you ever understand that I'm on your side? I'm on *your* side! And they are, too." His voice grew louder. "They care about you, for Christ's sake. You're not just a name in some hopper." He pointed a finger at her. "This is America. You can say whatever the hell you want to say. They might not like it, but nobody's going to . . . to *punish* you for it!" He slammed his fist down on the car hood, shattering the thin layer of ice that encased it, sending crystal zigzags radiating from his glove like distorted spokes of a wheel. "It's the Army's job—it's my job—to care for you. I do care for you! And you . . . treat me like a villain. Like a spy."

She did. That's how she acted toward him. Spiteful.

He didn't deserve it. Not him. He was innocent.

"Tom, I . . ." She shook her head, feeling suddenly weak and confused. "Forgive me."

He took her gently by the shoulders. "The war's almost over. You can stop now, Judy. You don't have to do this to yourself anymore."

"It'll never be over."

"It will. There may only be hours left. Go home and rest. You're tired."

CHAPTER 27

Tuesday, January 23, 1973

"GOOD EVENING," President Nixon said. "I have asked for this radio and television time tonight for the purpose of announcing that we today have concluded an agreement to end the war and bring peace with honor in Vietnam and Southeast Asia."

The war was over! Lord! Jubilation lifted Kevin to his feet, but his mother and grandmother remained where they were.

"Mom!" He gestured toward the TV.

She patted a place on the couch beside her, indicating for him to sit there.

". . . was initialed by Dr. Henry Kissinger on behalf of the United States and special adviser Le Duc Tho on behalf of the Democratic Republic of Vietnam . . ."

Why weren't they celebrating? He looked at Leona, who was viewing the President with careful attention. Had the war gone on for so long that they could not truly believe it was over? It was!

His mother crossed her arms, and Leona's rocking chair began a measured motion, the pose of people still waiting.

It wasn't over.

No matter what the President said, no matter how many treaties were signed, it could not be over for them until his dad came home.

And their vigil might last a lifetime.

Wednesday, January 24, 1973

"KEVIN! KEV!"

He looked back toward the school.

"I'll walk with you," Sam said, catching up. "Aren't you just freaked out about the war being over? That's great, huh?"

"Um," Kevin grunted.

"Jeez. You've been acting all day like you're going to your own funeral or something. I thought you'd be happy."

"Not yet," Kevin said tersely.

A book tumbled from under Sam's arm. He went back to retrieve it. He picked it up by a corner and—with exaggerated movements—licked the slush from it, purring. Ordinarily this would have gotten at least a smile from Kevin.

"I'm losing my touch," Sam said. "Maybe my timing's off." He studied Kevin thoughtfully. "Oh. Yeah. I get it. Not knowing could be better than knowing, right? If it's bad news."

"Right."

"That's a bear." Sam pursed his mouth to one side and then lit up with an idea. "What you need is a good stiff drink."

Kevin stood in Sam's kitchen doorway, watching him roll up his sleeves.

"Nothing to worry about. The owner won't be back from the beauty parlor until five. But before I make this potion, there are a few things you need to know. The recipe is a family secret. It has brought my ancestors luck over the centuries. It tastes rotten, but one swig and your greatest wish will come true. Your father will appear." Sam pried the top off the blender.

Kevin sighed. This would be something dopey, designed to cheer him up. Well, he didn't feel like it.

Sam peered into the refrigerator, removed a carton of buttermilk and poured some into the blender. "Ingredient number one." He brought out a couple of eggs and laid them to one side. Then, having extracted a box of Jell-O from a cabinet, he ripped the pack and ceremonially dumped lemon powder onto the liquid.

"Two eggs," Sam said slinging them in, shells and all, sending up a sticky spray. "Let me see." Sam opened the refrigerator again and dug through one of the drawers. "A clove of garlic. That's what gives it power." He dropped it into the mess. "And . . ." He held the blender under the faucet with a flourish. "Three-fifths of a cup of hot water."

A bubble of laughter rose in Kevin. He snickered.

Sam regarded him with disdain. "I must warn you to take this seriously." He set the blender on its base, fitted the top to it and punched "Puree." Eggs and garlic flew against the container in a yellow-brown tumble; the concoction spun itself into a jaundiced blob.

Sam produced a brandy snifter and filled it, jabbing a straw into the foam. "To your health, sir! And to the health of your father." He handed the glass to Kevin. "Drink up!"

Kevin wrinkled his nose, beginning to feel a giddiness overtake him.

"Well, at least have a sip. I went to all that trouble."

"What's it called?"

"You've heard of a Screwdriver?"

"Yes."

"This is a Can Opener."

Kevin hooted with laughter. "I'll bet!"

Thursday, January 25, 1973

"GREER, RONALD BRYAN," Kevin wrote, under the pale light of his desk lamp. *"Greer, Ronald Bryan."*

Greer, Ronald Bryan. Kevin's fingers throbbed with the effort. These three names had become litany in the last few days; when Kevin was not writing them, he was thinking them. Concentrating. He could make this name travel. He could force the Scribes of Hanoi to ink it onto their list, or he could make it magically appear in the correct alphabetical spot. Nothing could keep it out of North Vietnam, not the ocean or barbed wire or sentries. It was fishlike, swimming almost invisibly through air; it was graceful, flitting across parched afternoons, darting beneath moonlight toward its destination. The three names were spangled, slender, connected by silken cords. They undulated along a correct and fluid path. They were readable to all people, their language convincing and exact:

Greer, Ronald Bryan. Set This Man Free.

Saturday, January 27, 1973

MUST BE A wedding. Someone's car horn was making an awful lot of racket. Kevin left the model airplane he had been gluing and went to his bedroom window; it was on the side of the house, and from it, he could see for blocks.

One car was making all that noise! It was heading toward him, speeding. Now he could see. It was . . . Major Wellington.

It could mean only one thing.

The din of the horn was deafening, even with the windows closed. The car screeched into the driveway and glided up over the front lawn, leaving tire tracks in the winter-wilted grass.

Kevin heard his mother scream, a wild sound of thanksgiving and total unbelieving surprise.

The dizziness of a fast-moving Up elevator tore at his head. He pressed his cheek to the icy pane, an unnatural heaviness weighting him. There was a rustle as his grandmother hurried along the hallway. His mother fumbled at the front lock. *Thwunk, thunk. Swish. Bam!* The closing storm door jolted him into a run.

Judy had rehearsed this moment so many times. It had been a game to fall asleep with at night, instead of counting sheep. *Tom would get out of the car, beaming. No words would be needed.*

But daydreams were dangerous—they held up an ideal that could never be attained. She must be wary. Ready for the hidden thorn.

She stared as Tom swung himself out of the driver's seat, grinning.

A mirage. He would disappear.

Judy descended the front steps cautiously, fearing to look away from his joy. "Is Ron . . .?"

He saluted smartly. "On the very first list!"

"Aaahhhrrrrr!" Kevin wailed with glee as he ran along the sidewalk toward Sam's house. "Arrrrgggghhhhrrrr!" He hopped, flapping his arms. He could fly!

Sam was in his driveway, shooting baskets. He dropped the ball and put his hands on his hips as Kevin approached.

"Aaaarrrhhhgggrrrr!" Kevin hollered. Sam began to laugh. Kevin bounded at a telephone pole, bashing it with his shoulder. "Ouch-ouch, owwwww!" He stumbled toward Sam. "Victory! Power to the potion!"

"Your dad?" Sam asked, still laughing as Kevin charged him. "Your pop?"

Kevin took Sam down with a galloping tackle.

"He's coming back?" Sam said breathlessly as they wrestled.

"Yes!"

"Yessss!" Sam echoed, encircling Kevin's waist, squeezing, trying to toss and pin him. "Yessssir, boy! That ol' Can Opener . . . it works every time!"

CHAPTER 28

Sunday, January 28, 1973

JUDY SAT in a corner of her living room, amid bedlam: reporters and photographers noisily elbowing past each other to get to her. Hot television lights. Nests of wires and plugs.

It had started the evening before, and by morning there were so many people wanting interviews that Judy and Leona hadn't the heart to keep them outside in sixteen-degree weather. At dawn many of the neighbors—seeing the action—had baked coffeecakes and arranged them on the dining room table around a basket of red and yellow roses Carolyn Vincent had brought.

Judy had been awake all night, stunned and euphoric. Toward morning she had taken a leisurely bath and washed her hair, setting it carefully. It was a new beginning. A new life.

Still more cars and news vans were pulling up out front, clogging the street. A cab was stopping, near the front walk. Judy peered through the glass. Who? Connie Roberts got out, smiling, carrying an overnight bag and a big box of candy.

Connie and Judy sat on Judy's bed, eating chocolates and drinking champagne. A silliness had begun to possess them. Connie lay back against the pillows and crammed an entire candy turtle into her mouth. It was too big to chew comfortably; her cheeks puffed out as she tried.

"Impolite!" Judy teased, tickling her.

Connie gulped. Gulped again.

"You're going to choke to death!"

"Not before I take a lover!" Connie laughed.

The remark pricked Judy. *Grant was still in trouble.* "Nothing's getting any better?"

"The therapy's a waste of time. So far."

"I'm sorry."

Connie held an imaginary microphone toward Judy's mouth. "Tell me, Mrs. Greer, would you advise me to take a lover?"

"No comment."

"Judy." Connie giggled. "You don't say, 'No comment.' Hasn't the military taught you anything? 'No comment' implies guilt. You say, 'I am neither aware nor unaware.' Or you say, 'Let me get back to you on that.' "

Judy hefted the bottle from the carpet and dribbled its remaining champagne into their glasses. "Let me get back to you on that."

"I need help," Connie said. "Now look!" She dug through her purse one-handed to find a small notebook. "I intend to write down the name of the person who helped you." She poised her pen over a clean page. "Address and phone number, please."

Judy gave her a sideways glance.

"No secrets. We took an oath."

"That was a lot of years ago."

"You were in the greatest batting slump of all time," Connie said, crooking a finger at her. "And absolutely delirious to stop the war. And then—all of a sudden— everything went the other way. What changed you? *Who* changed you? Do I smell, perhaps, a little intervention— say, by Uncle?"

Judy sobered slightly. "You're off the deep end about that stuff. You've got me looking behind every tree."

"What about your airline ticket?"

"Sometimes I think you and I want to find a culprit. A scapegoat. So we'll have somebody to blame for what happened to us."

"Well, if you ask me"—Connie drained her glass—"it's an entire era of deceit. It starts at the top and comes right down to our level." She wrinkled her forehead in a pose of wisdom. "Wa-ter-gate. For instance."

"What does that have to do with anything?"

"It's not just an election prank, you know. It's a philosophy. Of this government. Get what you want, even if you have to cheat. I wouldn't be surprised to see that trail lead into the Oval Office." Connie raised the bottle to her lips and sucked at the last few drops. "McGovern never had a chance. It was like Nixon had a . . . gang . . . whose only job was to screw the other candidates. Ask me. I was there."

Off the deep end. She was.

"They walk among us," Connie whispered dramatically, leaning onto her elbows and crawling across the bedspread toward Judy. "They wear ordinary faces, but they stick it to us. It's like the combat boots Grant saw in Nam. Army issue. They had rubber insets on the bottom in the shape of bare feet. So that GI footprints would blend with the footprints of the natives."

"Well, first of all . . ." Judy got up to stretch. *Sheesh. Tipsy.* Her stomach sloshed; she tried to focus on Connie. "The military and the government are two different things."

"Not at the moment. You should be more suspicious. Like me." Connie gave her an openmouthed grin.

"You're drunk."

"Yes, we are. You know . . . I never think of things that happen as coincidental or accidental. I think of them in relationship to each other, tied together by an invisible string. I don't think you ever do that, Judy."

Why was she awake? Judy turned her head and looked at Connie, who was sleeping near her on a rollaway cot.

She'd been dreaming. A weird dream. About Grant. She could see him in his B-52; the cockpit window and his head were so little compared to the body of the steely, blimplike plane. He was flying over clouds. The doors in the bomber's belly opened, and tons of brand-new notebooks and ledgers and calendars and pencils fell out.

Allotments. Sure. What Grant had said about dumping fuel had become tangled in her dream with Susan's irate balking at oversupply.

But it couldn't be true. Imagine the waste, if it were.

Judy nestled her cheek into a cool spot on the pillow.

Suppose . . . just suppose . . . everything in the military were either conserved or wasted by absolute design . . . the ultimate machine in which all items—from paper to people—were deliberately and completely controlled.

The pink face of the man at Susan's party floated before Judy. The dog tag specialist. *Get rid of that shit. Don't send it home.*

Judy got up and put on her robe, slipped downstairs to sit in the living room, staring at a wall.

Greer? That your husband? They'd never let that one fall through the cracks.

I'm just telling you, they'll try to prevent it. There's hardly anyone who knows what he knows about China.

Intervention. Connie was so sure. And Tom was so adamant.

What if . . . they were . . . both right? What if she *had* been manipulated—but for the good of Ron Greer? And for the convenience of the Army. What if they had placed her in a kind of protective custody in which her life was made happier and her attacks against the government were curtailed? Two birds with one stone.

Ridiculous. How could they possibly have done that?

Monday, January 29, 1973

"Susan, this is Judy. Can you talk?"

"For a minute."

"See if you can find out Campbell's MOS."

"This is Susan Benson."

Susan. She was being so formal.

"In regard to your inquiry, the MOS number is one that cannot be traced."

"Everyone has a job—I'm just asking what his job is."

"I understand your concern. There is no MOS listed for the number in question. All inquiries regarding this number are to be referred to the Pentagon."

Wednesday, January 31, 1973

"I COULDN'T BRING it out with me, so I memorized it," Susan said as she finished laying nine paper plates across her kitchen floor and spooning dog food onto them. "I had a devil of a time getting it without signing my life away. You're lucky I have friends in high places." She opened the cellar door, and a tumult of puppies spilled into the room, hungrily vying for position at the doggie picnic. "It's just a background file, though. It didn't say what he does now."

"Let's see if I can remember it all." Susan put a hand over her eyes. "He was born in 1935—April second—in Franconia, New Hampshire. He went to high school in Hartford, Connecticut. He's got a B.S. from Amherst and two advanced degrees from—are you ready for this?—Yale."

"A Ph.D.?"

"In psychology. He's been married and divorced. Two children. Girls. Here comes the interesting part." She led Judy into the den and flopped down in front of a dwindling fire. Judy sat next to her. "He worked for the Chicago Police Department seven years before entering the service. The Army must have wooed him. He skipped lieutenant and came in as a captain."

"He was a policeman?"

"Fancier than that. A crisis mediator."

"What the heck is a crisis mediator?"

"Crisis mediation is a special area of psychology. Campbell took his Ph.D. in it."

"Well, what is it?"

"The crisis mediator is a real cool head; he calms down

people in tough situations. He's the guy who goes into a bank where some nut is holding everybody at gunpoint and offers himself in exchange for the hostages."

"Joe Campbell?"

"It listed at least half a dozen police situations in which he was the hero—a smooth talker. Kept people from being killed. At that time he was the only crisis mediator in the entire Midwest. I guess Chicago used to lend him out. Some of the incidents were like in St. Louis and Omaha. Judy, what do you suppose a guy like that is doing at Fort Harrison? He's heavy artillery. It's quiet as a tomb around here. The most dangerous thing that happens is the end-of-the-season sale at the golf pro shop."

A crisis mediator. No. Nobody was going to set something like that in motion just for her, just for the Greers. They were thought of as POW statistics—nothing special. Except . . .

. . . for Ron.

Susan looked at her quizzically and then with disbelief. "Oh, my God," she said.

Thursday, February 1, 1973

JUDY FORCED her way past Joe Campbell and into his house.

"Judy, what . . . ?"

She ran up the stairs to his loft, hearing him follow her. She would start with the desk. She yanked the three drawers out of it, one at a time, and dumped the contents on the floor. Rubber bands . . . a stapler . . . clean envelopes . . . an accordion file, labeled "Bills." She reached into its compartments and began pulling out the papers, setting them in a row on the floor.

In her peripheral vision, she could see Campbell's black Army shoes striding toward her.

Power bills. Phone bills. She opened a phone bill; there were no long-distance calls on it. She opened the next one.

Joe hunkered down next to her. "What in the world are you doing?"

She opened a third phone bill. There was one long-distance charge on it. Hartford, Connecticut. She folded the invoice and put it in her jacket pocket.

"Do you have a search warrant?" he asked.

She met his gaze. He seemed amused. "What are you looking for?"

She turned the bill file upside down, shaking it. Stubs from water company statements, receipts from grocery markets. Texaco Oil Company credit card purchases.

Judy got up and went to the dresser. The drawers were too heavy to lift out. She began to throw his clothing onto the bed. Sweaters, socks, underwear. There was nothing here. Nothing that could tell her what she wanted to know.

"Be sure you look behind the pictures," he said. "I might have a wall safe." He unbuttoned his shirt partway and pretended he was going to take it off. "Would you like to search *me*?"

She glanced at the striking green eyes, the dark, wavy hair, the tall, athletic build. Stereotypically perfect. No wonder she had been willingly misled.

She emptied the nightstand. Magazines. A box of tissues, a flashlight.

"What's this all about?" His voice had acquired an edge of irritation. "Judy!" She flashed past him and took the stairs rapidly. There was another desk in the living room; she began to rummage through it. A stamp collection. A pile of personal letters. From Joanne.

"Judy." She heard anger. "Stop it now. What is it you think you'll find?"

She stared at him; she wanted to see his reaction when she confronted him with his MOS.

"I want to find out why you're here. How much did the Army pay you to straighten out the Greer family?"

His eyes registered alarm.

"What is your salary, Joe? Two thousand dollars a month? Let's see . . . you've been here six months all together. That's twelve thousand dollars. The Army spent twelve thousand dollars on our mental health. That's cheap—isn't it?—to preserve the future of their star political scientist, the government's expert on China, to make sure he doesn't have any trouble when he comes home. They've already got his travel plans set up, his conference with old Mousie Tongue. You had me fooled with this . . . this movie set. Secluded. How convenient. *Give this woman a thrill. Comfort this woman.* Tell me, do you have to take acting lessons to get a degree as a crisis mediator?"

He had been listening to her as though he were formulating a rebuttal, but with these last words he put his hands up in a gesture of surrender.

"You son of a bitch," she whispered. "No wonder you can't cry."

He went and sat at the table with his back to her, his head bowed. For an instant a terrible misgiving seized her. What if it were all circumstantial? What if he were essentially a passerby—here on another confidential assignment—who became enmeshed in their problems, tried to help them? What if he had unintentionally grown to love her, to love Kevin . . . and Leona. Had his innate kindness kept him from interfering with the homecoming of an abused and lonely man?

No. If it were circumstantial, he would have seemed shocked by her accusations, baffled. He would have protested.

She came around the table to see his face. "You planted yourself in that coaching slot. Kevin needed you. *I* needed you. You got me that job at the museum. When I told you they had put me off, you pulled some strings, didn't you? How did you do that? How *did* you? How did you get so close to us?"

She sat in the chair opposite his; he didn't look up. "Another sensitive mission successfully resolved by the Army's crackerjack, top-secret counselor."

Betrayal. The most jagged of all wounds, the most unhealing.

"It all went like clockwork. We were so . . . desperate.

But you made a mistake on this one: You broke the paramount rule. You fell in love with us, didn't you? All of us."

He raised his anguished eyes to hers.

"Didn't you?"

He said nothing.

"You can't tell me, can you? You're a career man. The Army *first*. You have your orders. You're in agony, but you're going to play 'Taps,' no matter what."

A surge of anger burst through her, and she shoved the table at him, chopping him in the ribs with the edge of it, nearly sending him over backward in his chair. She pushed the table again, as hard as she could. It caught him in the side as he struggled to get free of the furniture and stand up.

He reached behind him quickly and, grasping the chair, set it aside. He had regained his balance now and was moving toward her. She would not let him touch her. If he had any true feeling for her, he would have told her. Long ago.

She smashed him across the chest with her fist. "Cry!" she said.

She hit him again. "Cry!" She couldn't stop striking him; she would make him cry. She *would*.

He did not defend himself; he stood quietly taking her blows until she could see that she was hurting him. And then he shifted away from her, holding her off with an outstretched hand until she stopped trying.

"Damn you," she said, exhausted.

"Come here." His voice was gentle. He reached for her.

She ran to the door, opened it; he put an arm across the frame to bar her way.

Judy glared at him. "Tell me!"

He studied her face intently, sadly, and lowered his arm to let her pass.

"You liar," she said as she left him. "You bastard."

CHAPTER 29

Saturday, February 3, 1973

"ARE YOU SURE you can get a ride home?" his mother called from the car as Kevin headed toward the roller rink.

"Sam promised me. I'll be back by dinnertime."

"Okay then. Have fun."

"Your tickets are all taken care of," the woman at the window said. "Go ahead in."

Justin's parents must have paid for everybody to come to his party!

Kevin crossed the lobby and approached the solid inner doors. Where were his friends? Perhaps he'd gotten the time mixed up; he couldn't hear the clatter of skates or the bumping rhythms of the organ music.

Kevin tugged the door.

The first thing he saw was the banner: CONGRATULATIONS, KEVIN. Then he realized the size of the crowd beneath it: several dozen kids, all lined up like a choir, their faces radiant with excitement. As he gaped at them, bewildered, they began to applaud loudly.

For him?

They were looking at *him!*

Someone in the back freed a net of helium balloons—red, white and blue. They floated upward in a rush, to bob along the ceiling. In the haze of people Kevin picked out Andy and Justin. And Sam, wiggling his eyebrows at him from the second row. Craig, Ray. Kids from school. Cindy Carmichael—a girl he liked.

The group broke and surrounded him with humming chatter.

"I'm happy about your dad," Cindy said, shyly presenting him with a balloon and giving him a pat on the arm.

Sam came forward suddenly and exploded the balloon with a straight pin. Everybody laughed.

"Those of you who need skates," Mrs. Helms announced, "come on over and get them at the rental counter."

Kevin put his head close to Sam's. "*Justin* thought up this party?" he asked.

"Yeah."

"Why?"

Sam shrugged. "He wanted to."

People were parading past, thumping Kevin on the back and handing him homemade cards. His gaze zeroed in on Justin.

Of all the . . . He didn't have the best of feelings about that kid. The guy had bent back and forth like a weed in the wind.

Justin put his hands on Kevin's shoulders. "I'm glad for you," he said.

A wisp of resentment formed in Kevin but widened quickly into peacefulness.

It was not a time to look back. It was definitely time to move on.

"Coach Campbell wasn't at the party. He's just sort of disappeared. The kids say they haven't seen him for a while. Does he know about Dad?"

His mother took the pan of cocoa off the stove and poured the steaming brown liquid into a teapot. "I'm sure he does."

"He'd read it in the paper."

"Yes." She laid their sandwiches and cups on the kitchen table. "Kevin, will you please tell Leona that supper's ready?"

"Okay." Why didn't Campbell call or something? His mom wouldn't talk about him lately. A guilt crept over Kevin. "Why don't we see him anymore? Was it because of what I said about him?"

"No, honey. He's been reassigned."

"He's gone?"

"I guess so." She set her mouth in the way he knew meant, *Let's close the subject.*

Kevin ached with disappointment. "But . . . he didn't tell me. I thought he really liked us."

"Will you please go and get Leona?" she said with finality.

Monday, February 5, 1973

A UNIFORMED MAN was joking with some kids on the front steps of the school. Kevin recognized him from the back.

"Hey, I've got to get going," Campbell said in a friendly way. He glimpsed Kevin. "I need to talk to my buddy over here for a minute." The kids gradually disbanded as the coach walked toward him. "How're you doing?" He smiled.

"Fine."

"I came to say good-bye. I'm leaving Indianapolis in a few hours. Just wanted to see you."

He *did* come! Kevin's throat began to close with emotion. Why did his mother think Joe Campbell didn't like them anymore? He seemed the same as always.

"My mother's mad at you," he said haltingly.

"I know."

"She thinks you never really liked us. Is that . . . true?"

Campbell inhaled and looked straight at Kevin. "No."

"Why does she think that?"

He coughed dryly.

Kevin was filled with the sorrow of Joe Campbell. It was large, painfully distinct. "A misunderstanding?" he said to let Campbell off the hook.

"Yes."

Kevin nodded.

The coach poked him lightly in the stomach, blinking. "I'll miss you. Take care now. Have fun with your dad. Treat him real well, okay?"

"Yes."

The man started toward his car.

Kevin's silence was choking his own breath out of him, crushing him. Hadn't he learned it with his grandmother? *Say it, say it.* He ran after Campbell, catching up with him and touching him at the elbow.

Campbell turned, solemn-eyed, and put his arms around Kevin's shoulders. Tight. So tight it hurt. Kevin hugged him back. They held each other for an eternity.

For a single, swift second.

Monday, February 12, 1973

THEIR HOUSE wasn't their own anymore. Strangers and friends and relatives were always in the bathroom or making coffee or taking pictures of them. Flowers were delivered, great fresh bunches of dewy daisies. Chrysanthemums. Elaborate dish gardens. Casseroles were brought in; the refrigerator was crammed with cake. People stayed overnight: his mother's friend Connie, Carol Lynn and Heather, Uncle Ed and Aunt Teresa. Notes arrived, and telegrams. The phone rang constantly. Newspapers wanted old snapshots of his dad. His mother no longer locked the front door. Kevin gave up on his homework. These were blissful days. He moved with them and hid among them, bearing a grateful astonishment. Everything he had wanted was now his.

Tonight the living room was full of guests: Major and Mrs. Wellington, Susan Benson, Uncle Bill. A man from the Indianapolis *Star* who wanted to take photos. They all were looking at the television. On its screen planeloads of POWs were arriving at Clark Air Force Base in the Philippines. Kevin knew these were films: His dad had been flown to Clark that morning and taken to a hospital. Time was all mixed up for Kevin—there was something like a ten-hour difference between Indianapolis and the far Pacific.

A few men were being carried down the airplane steps on stretchers. He hoped his dad wouldn't be one of those. He glanced at his mother and Leona, whose postures were stiffly apprehensive.

This could be bad, Kevin thought, an unforeseen disaster: injury, permanent and crippling . . . binding his father to the rooms of their house.

Leona suddenly tapped his mother's wrist. Kevin leaned forward, all his attention focused on the man standing at the top of the airplane stairs.

"It is!" his mother said in a foreign tone. "Isn't it?"

"Army Lieutenant Colonel Ronald Greer," the television announcer said. A whooping cheer went up from everybody in the living room. His mother clasped his hand and Leona's.

The man was coming toward them now, smiling, saluting. *Oh, yes!* This man had read him a thousand bedtime stories; this man had played tag with him in the yard. In this man was mirrored his own face.

It was his father.

Tuesday, February 13, 1973

"HELLO?" Kevin said.

There was a sputter of static on the phone line, and then a faint, windy roar as though he had put his ear to a seashell.

"Kevin?"

The confident voice moved things about in his chest, made them tremble; it reached back, back through the caverns of his life to touch his dearest memories.

"Yes?"

"This is Dad."

CHAPTER *30*

Thursday, February 15, 1973

JUDY SAT AT the dressing table mirror, trying to see what her husband would see this day. She felt like a bride: new clothes from the skin out. Pastel underwear. A lacy slip. A forest green wool suit, pearl earrings.

To him she was twenty-nine years old, with long hair and very little makeup. What would he think of the shag cut that fluffed around her face and lay in tendrils on her neck? She put her hands to her stockinged knees. What would he think of the shorter skirts? Well . . .

Unless he had changed a lot, he would not have strong opinions on hairstyles and hemlines. An extremely flexible man, Ron—whose tolerance was not strained by much. During the days of their togetherness she could have painted her face blue and he would have thought it interesting.

But.

Would he still want her? It had never occurred to her before today that he might not. In the ritual of getting ready in front of the truthful looking glass, a stark possibility had presented itself: What if he did not admire—in fact, condemned—the role she had taken against the war? He was, by his very occupation, on the other side of a formidable fence.

"The limousine," Leona said from the hallway. She stepped into the room with a smile of pride and approval. "You look so pretty."

Judy got up from the dressing table, experiencing a flutter of panic. *It could never be the way it was. Before.*

She gazed at her mother-in-law. From the oddly twisting passageways of marriage and children and three wars,

how could Leona have emerged in such serenity? Judy
had to know. Leona had to give her something she could
hold in the palm of her hand today like a brook-worn
stone.

"Tell me how you've done it," Judy whispered.

Leona took Judy's hands and pressed her cheek to
Judy's spontaneously, lovingly. "I have a very selective
memory," she said.

WRIGHT PATTERSON AIR FORCE BASE
DAYTON, OHIO

Jack Lowry systematically examined the two cameras
that hung around his neck. If there were any foul-up with
pictures of the Greer reunion, the editor would chop off
his head. He checked the film position, the ASA and F-
stops, the focus on both the normal lens and telephoto
cameras. He held his light meter up, toward the runway,
and read it again. He instinctively knew, from two decades
of successful—even prizewinning—photography, that his
equipment was completely ready.

He hoped the plane would not be late. The assignment
schedule in his pocket would challenge Superman.

He had staked out the best spot for this one; he just
hoped some fool wouldn't run in front of him during a
crucial snap of the shutter. He hadn't particularly wanted
this assignment. It was so damned far away from all the
other ones. Still, it beat the heck out of watching people
cut from car wrecks; it beat waiting while policemen dug
in the woods for a kinky-murder grave. A crusty edge had
formed on his sentiment over years of immortalizing life
and death on film. He knew that. But he had, quite
plainly, seen it all.

Judy sat in the limousine, at the edge of the airfield, with
Kevin and Leona and Tom. The windows were darkly
tinted for privacy, but she could see out very clearly.

Although security here had been fairly strict, a huge crowd had assembled—mostly uniformed military people; despite their numbers, they were orderly and quiet as they waited.

Joy was beginning to compress itself inside Judy like a wire spring; when release came, it would be a rocketing gladness.

Kevin pointed to a gray speck sliding in front of distant sun rays.

"Remember to smile," Tom told them. "He'll seem even thinner than he did on TV. Different. But try not to let it show. He's looking for assurance that you want him back. He needs to see it right away."

The plane was more defined now, following an arc toward the outer reaches of the runway.

"And let Judy go first," Tom instructed.

Ron Greer watched the enlarging airfield. There were throngs of people and a lineup of official cars. Judy and Kevin would probably be in one of those. His constant prayer had been for them. In his worst moments of physical and mental distress, he had found himself speaking their names.

He had perfect recall of his years with them; he doubted if there were anyone who could remember every scrap of time the way he could. The great blocks of monotony between the hours of terror had allowed him to reconstruct each event of his life: day-to-day detail he had thought it impossible to resurrect.

He had lived inside that. In those secret shrines. There Judy was a mischievous newlywed, handing him—for his shower—a cake of bath soap she had encased in clear nail polish. He had rubbed and rubbed at his wet skin, trying to lather up and then seeing her peek impishly over the top of the shower curtain.

Oh, to think that she still loved him when no letters had passed between them for six years! To think she hadn't even known for certain that he was alive. But she had waited. He would spend the rest of his days cherishing her for that. Cherishing their son.

What would Kevin look like now? That baby he used to cuddle; the boy who climbed onto his stomach every morning to waken him with damp kisses. That little boy ... He had been in prison for all of Kevin's elementary school years. He had totally missed the semesters of jack-o'-lanterns and puppets, of learning to read, to ride a bike. He had missed signing report cards and huddling on a blanket with his son under summer fireworks. Showing him the world, being a child with him.

A strange sensation had come to him at times in Hanoi: visits by his son as he grew. The delusions of a captive's wishful mind, perhaps. And yet ... he was so real ... the spirit of Kevin, just outside the reedy bars ... encompassing him with love and remembrance. His sore body would be calmed then, for many days.

Ron bounced lightly in his seat as wheels touched the runway. The plane's interior erupted with the din of hallelujah—the shouts and whistles and applause of free men.

He would live. Just live, he and his family. Whatever had come before would be put away. Done. There would be no second guessing, no judging of the decisions they had made in his absence. Trouble would be set aside. There was no trouble as long as you were free, as long as you did not have to bend to the will of a captor or be afraid each time a door opened. He had acquired a finely tuned appreciation. Even the feeling of his own feet at this moment, snug inside new socks and closed-toe shoes, delighted him. Sandals and a spoon had been his only possessions, forever.

He would leave the Army. Right away. Its intrigue and its endless categorization had ceased to interest him. A vision had come to him again and again, that of tilling the soil, the black, fertile earth of his country. Perhaps he would farm here in the flatlands.

And he would never leave America again.

The plane taxied to a halt. Men were straining at the windows for a glimpse of their people. In the confusion, Ron could not find his. *Let them be there,* he prayed. *Please. I love them so much.*

This would be the guy: Ron Greer. Lowry had seen some old clips of him. A real blondie. Scandinavian ancestors?

He centered Greer in the viewfinder. The man started down the steps; Lowry squeezed off a few shots and looked toward the family, who were waiting by a limo. *Steady. Get it. Don't miss.*

There he was! Kevin fought the impulse to run. His mother would go first. She was walking rapidly out onto the tarmac. His father saw her! Nowhere could there be anything more brilliant than the light of recognition in those blue, blue eyes.

Judy. Oh, my God. Precious soul. Judy.
He began to run.

He was thinner. Could he really be right there, right in front of her? *Smile.* She was smiling, she already was, smiling, it was so easy, smiling, smiling as she took him into her arms.

Suddenly it was real. Her softness, the scent of her perfume, her eagerness, the blending embrace. And here ... This must be ... Kevin! The boy leaped at him; he locked his arms around the child, kissing him on both cheeks, shaken and speechless.

A woman stood to the side, weeping. He turned his head and looked at her. His mother.

Lowry banged the pictures off as fast as he could. Powerful stuff. He was choking up. But he needed to keep the lid on for another minute or two. He wondered what the rookies would say if they could see the old man reacting to this one.

He lined up a crisp profile of Greer bussing his mom on the forehead. *Click.* Taking his son by the chin and staring at him, dazed. *Click.*

The family moved, arm in arm, toward the limousine. A good action shot—*click.* One could only guess at the trial these poor folks had endured.

Lowry moved with them and squatted to record their departure. The car doors were open, the people sliding in. Colonel Greer next to his wife. They kissed. *Click, click.* That would be a sweet one.

The doors closed. Damn. Tinted windows.

Lowry stood up.

The crowd suddenly interested him. He scanned it for a subject, a panorama. Women with handkerchiefs, babies waving flags. Too ordinary.

He switched to the telephoto camera, sweeping its magnifying eye slowly down the rows of faces.

Wait. Go back. Behind the skinny Air Force captain.

There!

He rotated the focus ring, unblurring a fabulous shot.

Paradox. That's what he went for: a stalwart, masculine face streaming with tears. It was almost too intense to be joyful; there was a touch of grief to it. Had he lost someone in the war?

Army. A major. With the telephoto he could read the name tag: "Campbell."

Yeah. Hell of a shot.

Click.